THE MIGHTY WORLD OF KRAK

Dermot O'Sullivan

Copyright © 2020 Dermot O'Sullivan

All rights reserved

The characters and events portrayed in this book are fictitious. Any similarity to real persons, living or dead, is coincidental and not intended by the author.

No part of this book may be reproduced, or stored in a retrieval system, or transmitted in any form or by any means, electronic, mechanical, photocopying, recording, or otherwise, without express written permission of the publisher.

ISBN-13: 9798664556193
ISBN-10: 1477123456

Cover design by: Art Painter
Library of Congress Control Number: 2018675309
Printed in the United States of America

The Mighty World of KRAK

Dermot O'Sullivan

DERMOT O'SULLIVAN

Contents

Rise & Shine
Decline
The Wantaway Blues
Whine & Dine
The Vision Thing
It ain't over till the fat man sings
Hope Springs
Daddy & Son
The Ritz Corral
Father's Advice
Up On The Roof
Madame Alone
Scheming
Boardroom Frolics
Progress
Mama, Mama
Reviewing the Situation
Past Tell
Up, Up and Away
Opportunity Knocks
Seconds Out
Bluffer's Luck
Afters
Hitting the Town
AWOL
Tempus Fugit
Reacquaintance
Madame Amiss
Sniffing Danger
Are we there yet?
Chief Gloater
Jittery Poker
This Mortal Coil
Pawn Moves
Deadline

A Lifeline
Plotters Everywhere I Look
Cat & Mouse
Tyrannosaurus Sex
Succession Planning
On The Eve
Into the Den
Valley of Death
Tempting
Oh, Oh!
Just a Nibble
Taking the Initiative
The Plans of Mice and Men
Satisfaction
A Message
Safe Harbour
Diversion
Vascher Reflects
Poised
Brought to Heel
Smokes & Mirrors
Foreboding
Rumbled
Things move quickly
Gone with the Wind
Squeeze Your Bum Time
The Noose Tightens
Teamwork
Girl power
All Things Must Pass
Epilogue
Appendix
   German Translations

DERMOT O'SULLIVAN

"The whole aim of practical politics is to keep the populace alarmed (and hence clamorous to be led to safety) by an endless series of hobgoblins, most of them imaginary." H.L. Mencken

RISE & SHINE

Dim Son presented a corpulent presence beneath the bell-curve of blankets, feather and down. The heavy tuft of greasy hair topping his pudgy face, continued its trail down the side of his head like a wet dishrag. He was coming out of a dream where he had grappled with a flying fish that slithered along the top of the mantelpiece. He brought the full force of a poker down on its body, drove it through the outer skin and impaled it on the wall, leaving a large gaping hole opened up on its side. He watched fascinated as the creature's mouth opened wide and a row of long narrow teeth, sharp as steel needles, manifested just as the fish expired. A kaleidoscopic stream of tiny, coloured flakes came flying out through the wound and filled the room just as two waiters, doing their best to avoid the sparkling shower, brought cloched plates of food to the table.

'Ah, time for breakfast number one,' Dim Son mumbled, 'those paper tigers are no match for me.'

Remaining in the prone position, he fumbled along the top of the bedclothes until his hand came upon the book with the black cover. He plucked it up and in one movement opened the top drawer of his bedside locker, slipped it in and pressed the drawer shut again.

Extended procrastination ensued before Dim Son arose and donned a purple-coloured satin dressing gown with the letters TGIF emblazoned in glaring gold letters on the back. After tying it loosely around his waist he waddled off to his personal gym, proceeded along the windowless passageway leading from his bedroom; the only illumination a multi-coloured strip of lighting embedded into the surface on both sides of the yellow parquet flooring.

The neon in the gym hurt his eyes and he blinked as he walked past a row of gleaming exercise machines, still encased in their plastic wrapping, and removed a barber's leather strop from its hook. On the handle it had, *The Uranus Strop, St. Louis,* printed out in ornate lettering. He flipped and twisted the strop, loosened up his wrist muscles and let it slide sensuously across the palm of his left hand.

The exposed posteriors of three women greeted him when he reached the small alcove at the far end of the room. The figures were bent over like yoga practitioners, their underwear down at the knees and their tops bunched up around their midriffs; fleshy rosettes, personally selected and presented by Madame Shoo who well knew his predilections.

    This morning she had laid out a small, a medium and an extra-large for him. He flicked the strop, remembering to concentrate on his rhythm and follow through. He started in on the S and M, using short warm-up slaps before he exerted himself, raising colour on the bare buttocks and the odd sigh of pain or pleasure - it didn't matter in the least to him. After he had got into the swing of it he moved on to the XL, now working the strop freely, with added vigour and aerobic intensity. He loved the real estate expanse of the XL and whipped faster as he heaved heavily, performing a dainty little pivot on his right foot, he came back around and slipped in a cheeky little backhand slice. Having amused himself with a few casual half volleys he started to move up and down the line again, occasionally lowering his aim and bringing the odd forehand smash down sharply on to the upper legs – that never failed to raise a yelp – and he kept at it until he felt himself stiffen. He glanced across the three reddened bottoms.

    'Eeny, meeny, miny, moe

    Who'll be first to get a go?

    Hmmm…medium rare is my mare.'

Lifting the silk dressing gown aside, he bore down on M and covered her, while riding to the accompaniment of pig-like snorting sounds. The heat from the toasted bottom underneath him added to his excitement and he kept it up until a triumphant shout of 'Bombs Away!' filled the room.

DECLINE

I'm sitting at my desk in the poky office - new workplace for the foreseeable - still in early as usual in the days following my demotion, but not out of eagerness or ambitious reasons I assure you. Those phantoms have long since departed. I am up at the crack of dawn most mornings and wander down from my living quarters quite simply because I have nowhere else to go and invariably find myself in the office well before I hear the patter of others along the featureless passageways of this static liner. Not that they come late – oh no – late is not something you are in KRAK; tip the cap and fart in your lederhosen if you wish, but late – or insubordinate - a no-no. Here the clever ones are whipped straight into the programme after school, while those less endowed but loyal are taken care of. Those clever but of questionable loyalty? – ahem – you better watch out... I've been watching out for quite some time now.

I am grateful, in a funny sort of way, that I don't have to attend the fat oaf's breakfast in the galley. All the *Fussvolk* have to be there of course while I can enjoy at my leisure the fine mokka sent over by Erika. I have no one to please and no one with whom to make dreary conversation; this is my happy moment. Nothing had gone wrong with the day so far and my resentments have not yet surfaced. They will, later in the afternoon, as the poison of another unfulfilled day seeps through.

One of the whippersnapper's first actions after he took over was to rejig the management structure and, as I feared, my working accommodation was relocated down to the lower management level on the third deck. Others moved up of course. You weren't officially demoted; they just gave you certain unmistakable messages, this inferior office for example, and let you decipher the communication however you wished. To be frank, there wasn't a whole lot of difference in the layout of the new place – quite a bit smaller to be sure - but it wounds nevertheless.

I get myself upright and head down to the scriptwriters' conference room, just next to the studio itself. Another new one this morning and she looks dangerously alert. Keen little buggers they are when they start out. Oh I well remember. Wait until they get to my stage. Don't ask me, they seem to change them around with ever-increasing frequency. Now, that other one, the male, the one who thinks he is *my* boss and is with me longest (and I know why!) introduces her, but for the life of me I cannot retain her name, something that sounds like a perfume. Looks intelligent though and that makes for a pleasant change. My friend starts to rabbit on about progress and I pretend to listen as he spouts out a set of instructions for myself and the new scriptwriter. Can be arrogant, that son of a bitch, but I know his game.

'Okay, point taken,' I interrupt, 'but hasn't there been surfeit of protest marches and banner waving in the most recent episodes? Are we overdoing it? Dim Dynasty Tales, in my humble opinion, could do with new impetus, don't you think?'

There was a hint of menace in my statement, most of it reflected back on myself I'm sorry to say, as it is well known that the viewing figures for the DDT TV soap opera (you daren't call it that BTW!) have plummeted. I am peeved I suppose; that lack of respect gets to me. God damn it, Chief Boddle Vascher used to share a bottle of the best with Daddy Kühl.

I get my silence, even if it isn't the one I'm looking for. The gawky fellow, sulks at having his verbal canter curtailed and retaliates with sullen aggression and snubs me with his upturned nose.

'*Wo sind wir denn hier*? Excuse me, where were we?'

No reply.

'Klusch, could you please remind us of the first principle of characterisation?' I ask, removing my glasses - not the wisest move in hindsight, as I have a somewhat weaker countenance without them – and I point at my aforementioned lanky friend, who, as I am too well aware, is a spy for KRAK's equivalent of our good old *Stasi*.

'Hmmm, hmmm,' stutters the *Spitzel*.

'Authenticity,' pipes up the new female, helping him out. A smarty pants, that one, I see; she'd buy and sell the other fellow.

Out of nowhere, an increasingly familiar wave of inertia hits me and I don't respond, veering off instead on an impromptu diatribe covering Motivation, Plot and Character, something I am liable to do at the drop of a hat, irrespective of which meeting I am at, or indeed which audience I am addressing.

'The first principle of plot?' I ask, following up my first question; the smug spy has irked me earlier than is usual.

'Eliminate the plottists and splittists!' the long string of spotty faced misery replies, his buck teeth exaggerating that sneering look of his.

I have to suppress a laugh. A brain-washed lackey - bound to go far. Thick as a brick. Simultaneously I notice the silence deepening even further. The new hire is getting nervous and

Klusch, his arms folded, not merely as a sign of disengagement but of suppressed rebellion, although he might not know that. I have confused him, and furthermore, rekindled his resentment at having to report to me, the foreigner. Oh I read his thinking alright. *Why was this stupid old foreigner, of suspect ideology, made Head of Creative? A negative leftover; the only thing he ever does is to run down every idea anyone else comes up with and he even has the cheek to dress differently.* I can smell the smouldering dislike and do what I usually do in that situation – invoke the name of The Great Invincible Father. You could bet on some movement in the chairs anytime Dim Son is mentioned. It is a type of reflex, ingrained; nothing to do with me really, but I know when to exploit it. And who can blame me? I wind up the meeting and set them a list of rapid-fire bullet points to contemplate.

'You can use my office,' I suggest, stretching back in the chair. 'Shall we say an hour for you to jot down some draft scripts; why not try something different? That would be nice.'

It takes a while for the angry flush on my bare pate to fade. I vigorously wipe my rimless glasses for some time, then change over to using my thumbs and forefingers for the grooming of my expansive walrus moustache. That settles me down; my ever-reliable worry bead as I reflect somewhat ruefully on my own situation. Back then, more than thirty year ago, I had bitten into something unpalatable, and here I still am chewing on it.

THE WANTAWAY BLUES

Gucci Gucci Gorby, that's why I had to stay. No doubt about that. Banjaxed everything, he did. I'll grant you it was no paradise but we had a system. Say what you like about it, a system that worked for most. Now look at the remnants. This place is run by an overfed, oversexed megalomaniac, it's piss poor and there isn't a hope in hell of anything ever changing. Yes Gorby's godforsaken Glasnost. No wall, no security. No security, no country.

Everything collapsing at home, so I stayed on here. I could have gone back but as a Cultural Attaché for the old regime, I'd be lucky to finish up working for the Goethe Institute... as a garbage collector. As an official state appointee, I was sure to be classified as one of its lieutenants and handled as such; interrogated I'm sure (they'd have called it a debriefing) as soon as I got home. In my darker moments I could even visualise show trials, standing in front of some judge holding up my beltless trousers, that sort of thing. My sister Erika was all the time encouraging me to come back, saying I'd be fine, but I didn't believe her. Well that's not quite true; I wished to continue supping at the table of the devil I knew.

Daddy Kühl's generous offer of the Chief Creative position for the DDT series on state television had its attractions, important job, close to the regime. How was I to know that he wouldn't live forever and I'd finish up with his Dim Son? Was I mad? A nincompoop who should be in diapers. My God, in Daddy Kühl's day, the parties were wild and there was plenty of Chivas Regal to go around. Let them drink Chivas Regal, ha, ha. I barely remember, or saw, the snotty-nosed young fellow back then. I have just one memory of him in Daddy Kühl's staterooms; a big kid crawling under the dining table trying to look up the women's skirts. Oh yes, I hear he has added spirituality now. I wonder how that will coexist with his carnal appetites?

Where does the time go? I had hardly excavated my nostrils when lanky Klusch, with whatshername traipsing behind, returned to the conference room. Some of their earlier enthusiasm had been restored, although Klusch's sidelong glance in my direction could hardly have been designated as friendly, however, the hostility of the earlier meeting was absent. He curtly informed me that the latest recruit was going to summarise for me. Fine. Let's see what they've come up with, probably the same old same old, I thought.

Well my friend, what a revelation that one turned out to be. Some smart cookie. I lay back in the tilting chair, gradually getting myself to an ever more horizontal position, not in the sense of dropping off with boredom; *au* contraire, I was positively fascinated as she reeled off basic premises and developing conflicts that took one from initial plotting to the scope of an epic fantasy opus. *VOW!* The creative writing courses must have stepped up since my day, but, as I was about to find out, it wasn't just that; I simply had one hell of a *Hellkopf* sitting across the table from me. All of this, I should emphasise, was delivered in restrained tones, juxtaposing conflicting stimuli and teasing out the evolving screenplay with the assistance of questions from Klusch and myself, until we finished up with a revitalised Vascher; for God's sake I was almost *begeistert.* I held back though, mumbling low key approval and threw in a few pro forma questions for good measure.

I would be keeping an eye on this one, and you know the strangest thing, and I swear this is the truth, I didn't experience a modicum of envy as I realised that I was in the presence of someone who surpassed my own not inconsiderable capacities. This was what I needed; this was *exactly* what I needed. *Ach, mein*

Junge, there's life in the old *Hund* yet. Even Klusch joined in and his hostility took a break as the three of us worked on tightening up character profiles and critiqued possible plot variations.

We might have spent the rest of the day at it if we hadn't been interrupted by an unusual flurry of activity in the studio itself, visible through the long plate glass wall which separated both rooms. The next-door occupants rushed around, opened the cupboard doors and dragged out large cardboard boxes and large plastic bags. They couldn't be retrieving the New Year decorations – they'd been packed away only a few weeks ago. Ubiquitous red and yellow banners bedecked with stars and strippers (I jest!), started to spill out on the floor. A minute later a messenger came in and dropped a letter on the table in front of me. Dim Son – TGIF himself - was coming to town. *Verdammt - auch das noch.* I'll have to go up and change into my tweeds. Got them from some Pixie Head on a stopover at Shannon Duty Free heading to Moscow for the Socialist Democratic Front conference. Oh yes, those were the days *mein Freund. Ausser Spesen, nichts gewesen.* The Russians attempting – and failing, I'll have you know – to drink me under the table.

I decided to take the stairs, to avoid banging into anyone, and the inevitable 'what's going on' questions; wanting to know if there was trouble brewing. What a question. This place was like a *Brauerei* – when isn't there something brewing? With a strangled laugh I appreciated the advantages of demotion and one less stair to climb. Flur S. Ence? Yes, that's it. What a fucking name; how am I supposed to remember that?

WHINE & DINE

On the bottom deck all non-management staff were assembled in the cavernous galley. Rows and rows of tables perched beneath coned light shades, the latter suspended from the high ceiling by long wires, stretched off into the distance of the immense room. The waiting diners stood attentively in front of their allotted table settings, an empty seat at each table. A sharp whistle blast broke the silence and echoed down along the room seconds before the lift door opened and The Great Invincible Father appeared.

There he stood, a vacant look on his face, his lop-sided hair seemed to pull his head to one side; an exotic animal caught in the spotlight. Shouts of 'Hail Father' went up with gusto from the assembled workers and went on until they were muted by another whistle-blast. The room was laden with fear, even more than usual, and Dim Son guessed that the news of the execution had already reached them. *Good.* The Yanquis might like the smell of napalm in the morning but Dim Son loved the tension when sphincter muscles were about to give way. The women in the room displayed toothy rictus grins, while the men gaped sheepishly, making sorry attempts at wan smiles. It was as if there was an invisible thread connecting each of the diners with Dim Son. He walked along the tables, randomly looking for one where he'd honour his subjects with his presence.

'Eeny, meeny, miny, moe…'

After breakfast Dim Son returned to his bedroom and took out the book he had put in the bedside cabinet. He then went into the study, an austere square room whose walls were lined with books, most of which Dim Son had never read. He had tried once or twice but usually cast them aside after a page or two. It didn't matter what: political treatises (the worst), heavy literature (no thanks), science fiction (passable), porn (better). Dim Son got more value from the magazines, especially the saucier ones he had delivered by the censorship office on the pretext of vetting what was coming into the country. However, the book in his hand, which he had taken from the Subversive section, was the only one he had persisted with and he settled himself on one of the two armchairs before the fireplace, crossed his legs and started to read from the dog-eared page.

'This is my body and this is my blood.' He didn't have to die, Dim Son thought to himself, he got that wrong; he had it in his hands; so close, almost perfect. Dim Son had no intention of dying, his interpretation of what he read was that *others* had to die; he would be the hammer, not the anvil, and by the great powers invested in him he was determined to take this a step further than the misguided guy he was reading about. How did he not see it: divinity came at a cost - to others; it manifested with the sacrifice – of others. That's the only way it worked. Life is tough and not fair. Dim Son's imagination started to fill with some far-fetched ideas and he chided himself for being bound by the limited vision of his father. He had a wider vision on which to fix his gaze; not just KRAK, but Mighty KRAK.

That night Dim Son cried himself to sleep as he did most nights. Clutching his old Teddy he rocked from side to side on the enormous bed, humming a keening melody. It reminded him of Hay Bama, who hadn't been around for years and now only saw when he made the trip up to the Blue Mountains.

She came in to his childhood bedroom and shushed him to sleep, her big hand on his forehead as his tears came down, hushing and keening in her masculine voice.

'Alright now Son.'

'I want my...'

Then it came, the whack across the face. Anticipated, and

at the same time a surprise.

'Shhh! Sleep now and all will be well again in the morning.'

Everything would not be well in the morning - they both knew that - but he knew what she meant. Now he had no Hay Bama. Madame Shoo had her uses, it was true, but these uses were confined to the provision of distractions and the boring logistics of state duties. Only Hay Bama could ease the pain, only Hay Bama knew its source. He resolved that it was time to see her again. It was a stressful journey to the back of beyond but there were ways to make it less unpalatable. The boil had festered up again and it needed to be lanced.

His tears ran out and dried sobs shook his jellied frame in the pitch-black room. Eventually, worn out from weeping and rocking from side to side, he dozed off and fell into a deep sleep. Dim Son was in repose, all was right with the world; outside the night watch was changing over; Dim Son was encircled by overwhelming physical security but the little foes between the ears occupied the citadel.

THE VISION THING

The introductions dealt with, a guided walk through the studio, a few short speeches from the heads of department, before we repaired to the conference room where I had earlier grappled with my ennui before the young lady, name… name… Flu…Flur S. Ence, revived me. Yours truly had been given the honour of leading the visit by a consensus of the studio staff, including that swollen-headed so-and-so of a director (there's your real reason for the failing viewership of DDT). This was one of the very few occasions when they respected my value and of course I availed of the opportunity to stick out my chest and make the most of it. There was but one agenda item: 'The DDT series and the future,' which I took to possibly herald more bad news layered on top of my 'demotion' but that was, as it transpired, off the mark – thanks to my good self.

After security had filed out of the room there only remained Dim Son and Madame Shoo at one side of the table and myself and the two script writers, both nervous, not the faintest whiff of cheek coming from that ear-in-the-door Klusch. The new recruit was quiet and looked as if she might have been trying to make herself disappear. Poor thing.

It very soon became clear that Dim Son wasn't going to speak or take part in the discussion and Madame Shoo, with her usual long-winded introduction and excess bowing in Dim Son's direction, made an opening statement on her ruler's vision, and a very simple vision it was; simple and totally absurd. I very nearly laughed outright there and then but my sense of preservation saved me. What Madame Shoo was saying was that the series needed to be turned into an epic, whose centre was the divine origin of the Dim dynasty. I also picked up – and no mistake about it - that this was to be presented as historical fact.

'I see,' I mumbled, reaching for my moustache and grooming so forcefully that I was hurting myself, 'I see, very interesting, a momentous…er, change of focus.'

Dim Son raised his eyebrows slowly, taking on the look of one of his bodyguard goons and I was struck with a (lifesaving?) burst of energy. Fear driven undoubtedly, as I pushed back my chair and paced furiously up and down the room. I could see that my script writers had assumed the ostrich position, petrified and convinced no doubt that I was about to take them down with me.

'Yes, Yes, YES!' Absolutely. Terrific. *Ausgezeichnet*,' I dipped into the mother tongue momentarily in my excitement and this brought a look of bewilderment to Dim Son's face. I knew I had to somehow pull this off; I was a man fighting for his life.

'I see it. Opening scene: The Magic Mountain, the double rainbow, the majestic Castorp peak, an illuminated beacon stretches to the heavens. A cry is heard, immaculate, immediately attended to by thunderous explosions in the distance, reverberating continuously in the background; even though it is daytime, a sparkling star, brighter than the Koh-i-Noor, can be clearly seen in the firmament, as Solaris waxes in the heavens...'

I looked around and, to my surprise, saw that they were still with me.

'The sounds intensify, deep rumbling sounds, the very earth is alive; we pull back in wide shot and buds and blossoms start to appear; magically, in *Zeitlupe – entsch...*excuse me, in slow motion and we witness a seamless transformation from winter to spring; music is heard – Daddy Kühl's Fifth Opus would be perfect - and the camera zooms in once again. We then come from above - the helicopter shot - and *there*, there we see it, the wicker basket, a soft focus close up, the swaddled infant opens his eyes, his hands clap, he smiles, he giggles. We cut to the raising of the national flag and the anthem fires up.

The melting snows create a mystic river winding its silken route downwards from the rugged peaks, conveying the basket with infinite care; it comes to rest, here where we are sitting, *right here* on the future foundations of the Ritz Corral. We add a few inserts, switching to the cities, towns and villages; people emerge from their houses and look skywards, their faces fill with wonder, children are hugged by their mothers, astonished fathers put their hands on their wives shoulders, Glory O, Glory O...'

I was out on my feet and had to pause for breath. I turned away from the table to conceal my exhaustion and reverted to moustache grooming, pretending I was deep in artistic contemplation.

'There you have it,' I croaked, as I swivelled round, somewhat recovered and just about made it back to my chair.

IT AIN'T OVER TILL THE FAT MAN SINGS

Dim Son was animated, striding up and down his stateroom, just as Vascher had done earlier on the lower level. Madame Shoo, seated at her usual spot in front of his desk, noted the contrast between the energised Dim Son and the flaccid figure who had reluctantly engaged with her on state matters earlier in the day.

'I didn't think the foreigner would get it.' He never referred to Vascher by name or title, a lingering envy, directed at Vascher's friendship with his father, smouldered on.

In a few short weeks Dim Son had gone from demoting Vascher – and to be blunt, that was the least he had in mind for the doddery TV executive – to now having to admit that Vascher had instinctively understood what he had in mind for the renewal of the Dim Dynasty Tale. He couldn't reinstate him just yet. Vascher would have to demonstrate his ability to deliver on his proposal and then Dim Son would have proven his wisdom in getting the best out of the burnt-out has-been.

'Does he have any wants?'

'Chivas Regal,' Madame Shoo replied.

'Send him a half case… regular vintage.'

HOPE SPRINGS

Madame Shoo had plenty of time to prepare for the interview with Chief Boddle Vascher as she sat at her desk thinking of ways to make the interview as intimidating as possible. After some contemplation she got up, with the nearest thing to a satisfied look on her face and moved the visitor chair back a few feet. Her desk was already on a pedestal and a foot or so higher than the floor; pushing the chair back further would have Vascher like a pupil in front of his Headmistress. Added to that, Madame Shoo was seated with her back to the window and would be in silhouette, while Vascher's every muscle spasm or blink would be visible, while her face remained inscrutable in the shadows. She turned and looked out the window before sitting down again, and as she did so, she opened her hands and pressed down the folds of her skirts in an involuntary movement.

I didn't know how it went to be honest. Was my dog and pony show going to be my downfall? Was I done for? You can imagine therefore my surprise at Madame Shoo's invitation. I hadn't made a fatal mistake - not yet. If I had, it wasn't a letter I'd get from Madame Shoo; oh no; a knock at the door (if that) and before I knew where I was, I'd be flying down the chute, bound for the putrid carrion heap at the bottom of the gorge and carried off in the river slime and sludge to Slag City. I breathed in and out – slowly and deeply. I was okay for the time being, but my anxiety I retained. I didn't know if it were Madame Shoo or himself I would be meeting, but I told myself to prepare for both eventualities. All through this I was unable to remain seated – even my moustache resented my twirling as I continued to pace up and down my cell, the damned tweed suit making me sweaty and increasingly irritable. This was a lot harder than breaking in new script writers. Well, lead on Macduff.

Blinded by the light, give me a break. What made her think I'd fall for that amateurish trick? Who did she think she was fooling? Chief Boddle Vascher, I'll have you know. He might be washed up but he knows lighting tricks when he sees them. Who introduced the modified *chiaroscuro* method to KRAKed TV I'll ask you once? Didn't think much of her White Balance; she should have got a *Profi* like myself to set the stage… that sort of carry on only works when you've got music and a petrified victim. Himself wasn't present and I cheekily opened the blind on the large porthole window at the side of the room. Madame Shoo and I go back a bit and I don't think she has ever forgiven me for being a confidante of Daddy Kühl, doing bugger all while she sweated with affairs of state. Thought she had me when I was demoted, but not so fast.

'A warm welcome Mr Vascher,' she said, greeting me formally in a voice without warmth or welcome. On the up side, there wasn't any menace I could detect, and I prided myself on a nose that was capable of sniffing out an underlying atmosphere. I also knew when to hold my feelings in check, knowing that danger might erupt from the tiniest of slip ups.

'Why thank you Madame Shoo for the great honour of receiving me in the offices of Dim Son. I can unabashedly state that I am genuinely humbled,' I replied, laying it on lardy, as *schmeichelhaft* as any Austrian, mustering as much unctuous sincerity as I could. She got the message alright. Madame Shoo was not slow, I will give her that. Personal Assistant, Office Manager, Chief of Staff (her official title, I'll have you know) to two dictators? I doff my fedora.

'Dim Son was most impressed with your synopsis of his

grand idea at the recent audience and he wants to move forward quickly with your proposal,' she said, having dropped all pretence at continuing with her top down approach to the meeting. I nodded, no, I bowed, almost to my knees and I can truthfully say that I was chuffed, I was bloody pleased with myself. I was in. *Jawoll!* Not only that, but a brown bag with bottle of Chivas was handed to me by one of her servants on my way out.

DADDY & SON

All through his childhood Dim Son was summoned once a week to his father's office; it was the only time he got to see him. He was seated at one end of an enormous table and instructed to wait quietly until his father had time for him. He did as bid and watched as people came and went to his father's work desk, supplicating, thanking, beseeching, explaining, but whichever it was, there was an underlying taint of fear that surrounded all visitors.

The only person who didn't give off this vibe was Daddy Kühl's personal assistant, Madame Shoo, as she slid in and out between visitors, escorting – forever escorting – and in between whispering quietly or talking in an undertone to Daddy Kühl, who listened intently to what she had to say. Dim Son was to form an opinion that his father didn't really pay attention to any of his visitors, but relied on what Madame Shoo's briefing, taking but a peripheral interest in the current speaker, as if just cross-checking that it aligned with Madame Shoo's counsel.

When the procession of visitors had ceased, Daddy Kühl looked over at his son and Madame Shoo also glanced in his direction. Both father and son knew it was time for their engagement, something that neither of them looked forward to. Their meeting coincided with his father's lunch break, or to be more accurate, the first part of his lunch break - later he went for a nap and after that he paced the lavish gardens on the top deck.

After Madame Shoo left the room, serving platters were brought by the catering staff and plates were filled with luncheon fare. Daddy Kühl sat in silence, as did Dim Son, whose appetite, even as a young lad, exceed that of the small wiry father, who wondered how he had begot this swelling balloon in front of him. This was Dim Son's favourite part of the meeting; he didn't have to engage with his father and he could eat as much as he liked, serving himself with large spoons from the bowls arranged around his seated position. He prolonged his eating, not just because of his excessive appetite but knowing that it cut into the allotted time for Daddy Kühl's lectures at the end of the meal, where he would have to nod and agree and, even worse, answer the awkward questions put to him.

Daddy Kühl, of modest appetite, uncorked his Chivas Regal and served himself a large measure and watched the boy spooning mounds of meatballs into his mouth – he never saw the lad show as much concentration as at table.

'Still struggling with the mathematics?'

Dim Son was about to shovel baked aubergine into his mouth and briefly struggled with the dilemma: whether to complete the transaction or to hold back and answer. With a rapid movement he stuffed his mouth and masticated noisily, giving himself time to consider an answer.

'Okay,' he muffled through the food as his eyes scanned for the next morsel.

The youngster continued to munch his way through an ornately presented cornucopia of food piled on plates and bowls while the elder concentrated on replenishing his drink, only occasionally taking a nibble at a morsel of food, selecting them as if on the lookout for the least distasteful piece.

'Mathematics is important you know,' he set forth in an imperial tone, knowing that he might as well be talking to the wall. His son returned a furtive look, immediately on the defensive, knowing that a lecture couldn't be far away. He didn't mind that so much, as it gave him time to eat and was preferable to the stilted dialogue where he couldn't keep his mouth filled in case a sudden question was thrown at him.

Daddy Kühl didn't disappoint and he shoved back his chair from the table, took his replenished tumbler of whiskey, leaned back and crossed his legs before setting out the many benefits of mathematics, not least the concrete realisation of KRAK's breakthrough SCUT-r technology, the latest development in the country's rocket programme. Dim Son spotted his opportunity and slid a few of the food vessels from his father's side of the table and swapped them over with his own emptied ones. The father spoke and drank while the son ate and munched. The meal finished as it usually did, with all plates on both sides of the table cleared of food.

'Remember what I have taught you,' Daddy Kühl intoned as he rose and departed for his siesta.

THE RITZ CORRAL

The Ritz Corral lay on top of a gorge in a line between Slag City and the Blue Mountains to the north. It was situated about seven miles from the former, a sea port and nominal capital in the south east but the construction itself faced the opposite direction, towards the mountains, although these were a substantially longer distance away.

For the few it was the Ritz, for most it was a corral. The top of the gorge was straddled by a natural bridge several hundred feet thick and, after he had cemented his control of KRAK, Daddy Kühl decided to build his folly there. Its shape was that of an enormous oceangoing cruise ship carved out at the top of the gorge, its stone prow cutting through the mass of rock, the seagoing analogy completed by the installation of port hole type windows along the length of the edifice.

Deep in the subterranean holds of the static liner were the coercive tools of power: secret police, rocket scientists, munitions, jail cells and right in the centre, enormous horizontal steel gates that dumped the Ritz Corral's waste – including human – into the Siouxer river down below from where it made its way to the polluted capital.

All was in order at the Ritz Corral; life ran smoothly and the eternal cycle ticked along. It may be an exaggeration to say that all was right in this world, but what world exists where all is right? In the Ritz section of the building, facing out towards the edge of the bowsprit, were Dim Son's sumptuous quarters, surrounded by security and every service one might ever wish for, provided by servants who lived lives in comfortable fear and watchfulness.

The top deck or flat roof of the building was divided into three main sections of roughly equal size: on the city side was the Market, where produce was shipped in and made available to the Ritz inhabitants; a 'People's Park', a forlorn concrete dominated open space, was in the centre, and on the northernmost section, facing the mountains, was Dim Son's Celestial Demesne, bounded from the rest by the DMZ, an area similar to the customs area in an airport, through which all persons and produce had to pass into the Foreboding City.

FATHER'S ADVICE

'Chou Late. In your first 40 days, mind you,' he had admonished Dim Son from his deathbed, this wheezing skeletal figure,. 'Understood,' he had replied, sneaking a few liquorices from his pocket, stuffing them along the outside of his gums, not just to savour that sweet taste circulating around his mouth but to block out the overpowering antiseptic smell in the room. The chewing could be done at opportune moments, and there were plenty of such moments, with Daddy Kühl grasping for breath and slipping into unconsciousness at regular intervals.

His head was like a pigmy's skull, covered in an almost transparent yellow skein of outer parchment, dried out and giving the impression that it could crack at any moment. The teeth had become more prominent and appeared to want to get out, the cavernous enclosure of Daddy Kühl's mouth looking too small to contain them. Snot hung at the bottom of his nose, being lightly shook by the weak breathing.

'I can't help you anymore,' Daddy Kühl had said, 'you'll find your own way if you first accomplish what we have set out in Part I. If you don't, well then you won't be long in joining me.'

That was Daddy Kühl at the end, an image that remained in Dim Son's head. Part I was complete; Part II, putting his own imprint on proceedings, was underway. Dim Son's eyes narrowed at the recollection, the very last words his father had spoken to him. What had they meant? Could they be tied in with the resurrection he had read about in the Little Black Book?

UP ON THE ROOF

Using Lift 4 to the top deck meant I avoided most of the madness of the market place and Pillar 8 was where the Peoples' Park started. I glanced down along the market before turning away, taking in the slanting stalls with their colourful stands of fruit and vegetables, spices and nuts, gewgaws and miscellaneous utensils of plastic and tin, each one manned by an enthusiastic vendor. The shouting and bartering between seller and buyer continued unabated, a well-stocked city centre market to all intents and purposes. Even those who sold here – though they had to be clear of the premises by curfew – were part of the elite, favoured by connection, bribes, or both, that allowed them to trade in the only place in the country that had disposable money.

I decided to go up on the roof on my way back from the interview with Madame Shoo. I needed to clear my head and standing or pacing on the roof of the Ritz Corral was the only place to get away from the incubated madness that buzzed on the lower decks. Up there I could take in the mountain peaks – the main range being hidden by the wall that sealed off Dim Son's private area, where, naturally enough, the panoramic views were to be experienced. A whiff of nostalgia and resentment flashed through me. *Laß es sein Vascher!*

There was no point in looking in the other direction as the enormous, star studded chimney in the middle of the Ritz structure, blocked out everything, perhaps no bad thing, as one was spared the festering mess of Slag City down below.

I had picked up some hints from my conversation with Madame Shoo; hints, if I had correctly interpreted them, that indicated that we were on unexplored and by implication, dangerous ground. She used the word 'we' but I knew she really meant me. Madame Shoo was adapt at survival and more than that, she had a finger in all the dykes around here and was rarely if ever in the dark about any of the goings on. What I did not know at this point was that she was still finding her way with the young fellow, and I reprimanded myself for failing to have seen that. On a positive note, I had made my pitch and I was positioned - sort of - to deliver what I had promised, but there was a great deal of steering by the seat of the pants in the new situation.

I had a pleasant walk of no more than 30 minutes before I

reached the northern perimeter of the public park. There I sat on a pre-cast bench and took in some fresh air. I should get out more often. How long had it been since I was outside? Six weeks? No, longer, *drei verdammte Monate* since I had been in God's air. What had got into me lately? I knew the answer to that one only too well and had ample time to contemplate the unexplored direction I was taking. Had I any choice? Not really. This was my last hurrah. Not taking up the cudgel would have seen me continuing down the line of more demotions and humiliations. There was no way Dim Son would let me immigrate back home or anywhere else, even if I had wanted to.

So I had to make the best of it. I summed up my position and noted the advantages that had accrued to me because of my decision to fight on. For a start I had regained one thing – an unfettered authority as Chief Boddle Vascher. There was to be no more sulking or insubordination from Klusch and I saw an opportunity to cement my dubious authority. That young lady had potential, brains to burn, and could be an asset in my quest. Then, as if the Blue Mountains had sent me a message through the clear air, I knew in an instant what I had to do: get Klusch involved in some sub-project or other, some long-term research role, anything to get him out of the way. What was that new scriptwriter's name again? Yes, that's it; simplify the whole shebang, and then see how we get on after that. *Meine Gute,* I was almost feeling productive. The ball was clearly in my court now, largely due to my own *Darstellung.*

I continued to think as hard as I could, even if it exhausted my underutilised brain and became the harbinger of deep weariness. Images of the broad sweep of the revised series came into my head – no problem there – however, another issue that I couldn't quite grasp, something out of reach, something requiring even more thought, kept niggling at me. I could get around the chessboard and survive on my wits – as I had done up until now – and see how far they took me; they had been of some service so far, even my greatest detractors had to acknowledge that.

My reflections were interrupted by a breeze, fresh and packing a punch, which blew across my face and I became aware of my surroundings again; the hubbub coming from the market in the distance and the twirling and tweeting of song birds behind the high wall.

That new one, she was smart. Would she have the capacity to assist me getting through this chapter of my earthly existence? If what I have in mind works out then it might even help sustain this mini revival, if that's what it is I'm experiencing. How to go about it? I'd definitely have to decouple her from that *Spitzel* Klusch, of that I was never more convinced as I headed back down. His connection to Madame Shoo and the shadowy apparatus in the *Hintergrund* wouldn't be any help at all. Of course, you may say that as Chief Creative that it is within my gift to do as I please with the department's staff, but you would be wrong there.

MADAME ALONE

Madame Shoo was knitting in her own apartments, ruminating on the earlier meeting with Chief Boddle Vascher. She had her best thoughts while her fingers were whirling and twisting through balls of wool; something tactile in the material, something soothing and contemplative in the activity. Developments had rebounded rather differently than she anticipated, but setbacks and difficulties were her bread and butter. While she acted with utter discretion with members of the management team, even with those whom she was certain were for the drop, she still struggled to credit Vascher's upturn in fortune. In line with other Daddy Kühl's confidantes, he had been squeezed out of the inner sanctum, something she felt was long overdue, and she could not remember one instance where a resurrection had followed such a downgrading; the opposite was usually the case, often at the disgraced manager's own hand.

She knew that Vascher was on probation, but who knew what the outcome of the proposed production would be? If the eminent bluffer succeeded - though she doubted that he would - then it would not be in her interest to be labelled a naysayer. She also had to acknowledge that she was still trying to find her way with Dim Son, and in his elevated role he had become an unfamiliar quantity to her. She had only ever seen him lounging about the place and disporting himself, that was if he wasn't gorging himself, and here he was in command.

It should have been a seamless transition – it was clearly coming – but it was not turning out that way. He simply wasn't up to the job (and neither was Vascher, but that was another matter); she couldn't take anything for granted and especially not her own position. Her thoughts, based on her own preservation instincts, absorbed her for some time and eventually she concluded that it was best to do as she had done forever: go along with it, see the road ahead before others did – a discipline that had ensured her survival to date.

She could even perceive uncomfortable similarities between Vascher and herself and that thought sent an involuntary shiver through her. So, she would continue as before, as if nothing had changed, turning up each morning in Dim Son's apartments, her clipboard with the daily activities and a look of intense curiosity on her face. When she examined it, she understood where the shiver came from. What if she didn't turn up, what if she didn't show due deference, and do a Vascher, getting away from responsibilities time and again? And the newly anointed Dim Son, did he want her around? Then remembering Dim Son's special request for the upcoming Executive Conclave, she put away the knitting and went to the telephone.

SCHEMING

'Good day Flur S Ence. Could I take a few minutes of your time?' I asked, having at last succeeding in learning her name off by heart and seizing my chance on the dreary ground floor corridor after a few days surveillance of her movements.

'Sorry… of course,' she looked taken aback but recovered quickly, giving me a half smile.

'Whatever suits,' I pretended to be in an absentminded fluster, 'just seeing you there has given me an idea I'd like to run by you. The meeting with Dim Son's went well,' I continued, determined to keep a rapid pace, 'I have had a follow up clarification interview and it would appear that we have the green light from on high. In fact I can be so bold as to say - we have got the go official ahead!'

In fairness to her she didn't squirm or fawn, but considered an answer before replying, 'It was a good presentation.'

'Why thank you, that's most pleasant to hear. I do need the team to understand where we're headed.'

'Will you be meeting the team?' she asked.

That caught me off guard. Would I be meeting the team? No I would not, not before I had decided what I wanted from any such meeting.

'Some planning needs to be done before we're ready for that, I think... and that is the very reason I am so glad that I came across you. Could I trouble you for a few minutes to share my thoughts?'

'Should I ask my colleague to come as well?'

Trying to remain as nonchalant as I could, I mumbled, 'Yes, perhaps... but later on I think... as I say just an informal chat is all that's required at this juncture. What did you think yourself?'

I had her there. I knew she couldn't flatly contradict me - and she didn't.

'I suppose... I mean, yes...and you want me to meet with you?'

I told you she was a clever clogs. She was just checking that she had heard correctly and didn't risk assuming anything until she was perfectly clear as to what I was looking for.

'*Genau*. Whenever you have a few minutes drop in to me. You know where my cubby...office is? Third deck, room 101.'

'Yes Chief.'

I turned to go, calling over my shoulder, 'I'll be in there for the rest of the morning.' No point in leaving it as an open invitation. Vascher be bold!

BOARDROOM FROLICS

The boardroom was prepared for the Executive Conclave, a regular high-level status meeting where the regional commanders reported directly to Dim Son on the situation in their personal fiefdoms. The boardroom, a small theatre-cum-cinema in Dim Son's quarters, was set up as if for a shareholders' meeting, with a sturdy mahogany desk standing alone on the stage, laid out with vases overflowing with red and yellow tulips. As there were only 12 commanders in attendance, the balcony area over their heads remained closed off and they sat directly underneath the overhanging plinth directly above them. The balcony entrance, protruding somewhat like a mini stage, was covered in purple drapes and had two uniformed guards standing perfectly motionless at either side of its entrance.

Madame Shoo was checking that everything was in order on Dim Son's desk - who had not yet arrived - ensuring that copies of the reports, laid out according to speaker, were placed conveniently for his perusal, should he wish to consult them, although she knew he wouldn't even notice them. The commanders below her were engaged in muted conversation, the usual air of uneasy tension hanging over the gathering.

The wrong answer, an unclear description of some event, Dim Son suffering from a head cold - any of these or other trivial events could trigger an outburst of venomous bile, ending who knew where. A tap on the shoulder on the way out and, quite possibly, the unfortunate individual might never be seen again. The commanders had learned to live with the uncertainty – they had no choice – and they weren't too slow themselves in meting out punishment. They became survival experts – the ones who were still there that is – adept at doing whatever was necessary to remain in the fold; the outer darkness did not bear thinking about. Execution was the least painful option and suicide by far the surest way of avoiding a downfall, providing one's reading of the situation was accurate.

A tragedy of course when someone topped himself in the mistaken belief that his days were numbered. That made matters even worse as Dim Son immediately instigated a purge, convinced that the deceased was part of some secret plot. Everyone then suffered. It was far wiser to keep a tight knot of survival solidarity going and to avoid losing one's head by any one of the multitudinous opportunities to do so.

Madame Shoo detected an atmosphere even more sombre than usual in the whispering below her and she knew why – the old guard had being gradually pruned. Dim Son had decided that loyalty to Daddy Kühl wasn't the same thing as loyalty to himself and refreshing the management team benefited him in several ways: a new set of people who owed their position to him and him alone; it kept people on their toes as others dropped around them. It had to be surgical, giving some the illusion that they weren't disposable, otherwise they might have concluded that they also had nothing to lose.

'Never take on a man with nothing to lose!' Daddy Kühl had warned him, 'such a person is capable of anything.'

Survival to the next Executive Conclave became a goal in itself and not a single one of the commanders had anything else on the horizon of hope as regards their continued usefulness.

Madame Shoo came up to Dim Son, who had just appeared on the stage, and a brief whispered conversation took place, Madame Shoo pointed to the entrance on the balcony above, while Dim Son nodded. She looked at her watch and left the stage after banging the large cow bell – a gift from the Confederation of Helvetia - on Dim Son's desk. It went quiet immediately and then one of the attendees arose with much coughing and shuffling and commenced his speech, full of facts, figures, forecasts, goals, achievements and aspirations. Dim Son wasn't listening but focused his gaze on the speaker, a glare which increased the man's nervousness to such an extent that sweat trickled down his face.

With 12 regional commanders, that amounted to three hours of speeches before the midpoint break. About half way through the first session, Dim Son checked his watch and nodded up at Madame Shoo, who was now on the balcony between the guards and not visible to the assembled commanders. As soon as Dim Son looked in her direction she went back out through the curtains and a few minutes later a scantily clad leggy female replaced her on the balcony. She had on a type of cape, pink in colour and transparent. Her breasts were bare and they only other clothing was a skimpy thong.

She had Dim Son's complete attention as she danced a silent seductive dance on the balcony, twisting and turning provocatively as the speech below her droned on. After gyrating for some time she turned around and shook her buttocks in the direction of Dim Son. His excitement grew and he hid his hands underneath the desk. The dancer removed the thong, catching their edges with thumb and forefingers and easing them down over her rump, all the time twisting and writhing until they reached her knees and she let them drop before stepping out.

Dim Son shuffled on his chair and the current speaker started to hyperventilate, convinced as he was that there was something about himself or his speech that Dim Son did not approve of. Meanwhile the lady on the balcony picked up something resembling a baton and playfully slapped her buttocks with it before rubbing it unhurriedly up and down between them, simulating a violin player producing soulful romantic notes. Dim Son was visible moving in situ and the speaker was near his wit's end, almost hoping that soldiers came and dragged him away.

Dim Son slipped forward on his seat as the speaker stumbled over the end of his speech and for the remaining morning speeches remained slumbered at his desk, possibly dozing or even sleeping. Madame Shoo in the meanwhile, had silently ushered the young lady back through the curtains as the drone of speeches continued. The guards' eyes remained straight ahead; they hadn't moved an inch during the performance.

PROGRESS

She was quiet, looking at me as she struggled to conceal her puzzlement. We were in my office, pressed on top of one another in the restricted space. She sat diagonally across from me, on the bare wooden chair at the corner of the desk. I had no storage space for the stacks of books, documents and miscellaneous items from my former office and I had dumped them wherever space was to be found in the new cubby hole. My previous office had a rather generous statement but, as you know by now, it only upsets me to recall those images.

    I was flustered and a teeny bit embarrassed. For one thing the physical confines of our positions were at the very least uncomfortable if not embarrassing – I could practically see down her throat and whenever she leaned back I was looking up her nostrils *um Gottes willen*! Not that the proximity was in any way unpleasant; *au contraire*, there was a most pleasant Nordic summer freshness coming from the person of the petite Flur S. Essence. My agitation persisted however, possible something to do with my guilt at the low level subterfuge I had used to get her into my office in the first place.

Shyness was to be anticipated – she was a subordinate and had not been in my office prior to this - and I assumed she had not even been on my deck; looking at her face I could also see a sliver of relief, as if she wasn't feeling as uncomfortable as she might have in the, for her, elevated clime of a higher deck. Nevertheless, she had placed herself daintily at the chair's edge, as if ready to be off at any moment.

'Thank you for coming,' I opened, not quite knowing how to get to the nub of what I wished to impart. She nodded, thinking I suppose that I had more or less ordered her to be here.

'You are most welcome to my humble abode, I continued; there is no need for any anxiety, nor should you feel under any compliment,' and for some unknown reason I couldn't resist a cheeky addendum, 'who knows, you might be the next Chief Creative!'

This made her blush and she looked at me as if I were slightly mad.

'No, it's not a joke, there are many turns in life. We do not know what lies ahead, isn't that the very truth of living?

She nodded again.

'Everything starts small,' I continued, warming into the groove of my philosophical proclivity, 'everything, from the acorn to the aged oak. This is clear, *ja*?'

I could see that she was beginning to relax a little more. That was good. I needed that; without her – or someone else's cooperation – I was unlikely to deliver on my promise to Dim Son et al. Just remember, I said to myself, don't frighten her off and before you know it we'll be up to our oxters in scripts and right down to the shooting sequences.

With that in mind I reverted to my usual waffle with the sole purpose of keeping Flur S. Ence on side. She listened politely as I continued for some time, regurgitating my ideas and proposals for the project. I was happy enough with progress and I continued my patter long enough to prepare her for what I really wanted to impart.

'To summarise Flur. S. Ence, I am most indebted to you for your visit here today, a visit that has helped me to clarify in my own mind the broad strokes and epic sweep of the upcoming assignment. It is an enterprise of breath-taking, not to say, daring dimensions – would you agree?'

This time I let the suspense build, holding myself back – not easy – until she should say something that validated my continuing approach – or not.

'I'm a little overwhelmed by the scale of the new production,' she said, emitting it in such a clear voice of honesty and concreteness that I had to gulp and my eyes watered for some reason. Was she right? Was she what! For a full second I realised the enormity of what I had let myself in for. I recovered and, feeding off her honesty, managed to throw out, 'too big for us, you think?'

What I liked about this young woman was that she wasn't afraid to think, and think deeply - something that perfectly complemented my own approach.

'No, not too big... but we cannot execute using the methods we have been using.'

My ears cocked up. I liked this. This was the way to get places! I kept quiet though, knowing I would get more that way from that superb little brain sitting across from me. And my strategy worked. She relaxed and reeled off a string of sensible ideas, all of them practical and eminently doable. I can be humble, believe me, but this girl mapped a way right through - from concept to canvas - the quest we were about to embark upon. It would have taken me months, and that is to suppose that I was even capable of reaching her level of analysis, to come up with what she was espousing. She had me listening, *listening* I tell you. And best of all, I now saw the perfect opportunity to separate her from that meddlesome *Spitzel*.

'Excellent,' I concluded, holding back my deep wish to

use her first name, 'I think we're beginning to see the elements of the structure emerge. I am most happy with this discussion. Perhaps we could turn this a regular session, let's say, hmm… daily? How about that?'

MAMA, MAMA

A visit to Hay Bama was overdue. Dim Son could tell by his demeanour and lack of energy; lethargy had set in and neither food nor call girls could supplant a deep need he had to renew and reinvigorate. This he knew instinctively but if you were to ask if it was a part of his awareness, then the answer – indeed the question itself – was unknown in his conscious world.

'I must see Hay Bama,' he called out in the empty library, while leafing through one of the glossy magazines. He stood up and cast the magazine aside and paced between the bookshelves.

'Get some hunting in as well. Yes, that's it. I'll summon to Madame Shoo and get my diary cleared.'

At that moment a feeling of appreciation for Madame Shoo passed through him and he thought she was the best thing he had inherited from his father, but Dim Son's memory could be very short indeed.

REVIEWING THE SITUATION

Flur S Ence was intrigued but not overly discommoded after the strange meeting with Chief Boddle Vascher. It had taken her a while to get used to the unpredictable ways of the media department and this went down as yet another example of its randomness. She knew she lacked experience but her confidence had grown as she settled in and delivered script after script to order. That was her way; concentrate on the work and let the peripherals, distractions mostly, take care of themselves. In that sense she was more than happy to leave Chief Boddle Vascher stride across the plains, tilting at the windmills and the multifarious phantoms he encountered. She didn't understand him, nor did she know anything about the convoluted history of the media department and his role in it, and she sensibly decided that it was none of her business.

Unbidden, her parents came to mind and she felt an ache, a longing for the simple love that existed in their modest hard working household. Being classified as a child of exceptional ability, she had to suffer the early severance of the familial bond, trust as she was into the elite school reserved for the regime's brightest. She herself might have preferred helping out behind the counter of the corner shop.

Unexpected as it was, Vascher was the next image that surfaced in her thoughts and she felt an emotional pull of some kind, fleeting and all as it was. Behind the bluster she intuited the milk of human compassion in that strange personality.

She was taken aback at first when the Chief stopped her in the corridor, but not for one second did she suspect that he had reconnoitred her movements for a few days before making his approach. She was a little overawed at being in a one-on-one conversation with a high ranking person; Flur S Ence thought the Chief was high ranking even if the man himself did not think so.

Still, her logic deduced, inviting her to his office, unforeseen as it may have been, had a plausible logic and did not breach KRAK protocol; so she saw nothing unusual in it - he was her boss after all. She was a by-the-book person and if there were any slight misgivings about the meeting it was to question the absence of her teammate, but, as she could not know, Vascher's motivation for the meeting was to plot around that very obstacle.

Flur S Ence didn't know what Vascher wanted from the meeting, as there was no realisation on her part that he feared being exposed and, worse, did not think he could pull off his grand gamble without her cooperation. The meeting with him did however help deepen her understanding of the changed circumstances of the DDT series, to the point that she received an insight into the true scale of what Vascher had taken on. She also detected the risk that went along with the project and, knowing that Dim Son himself was the instigator of this initiative, she was fully aware that failure, as everyone knew, was more than an orphan in the land of KRAK.

Vascher's sudden enthusiasm was a bit of a surprise, as he had been remote and uninvolved in recent months. She didn't listen to rumours so didn't know any of the details of his silent and unannounced demotion; but she did notice Vascher's trajectory had taken a sharp downward spiral in the weeks before the crisis meeting. Everything had changed after the meeting with Dim Son and here he was leading a rescue mission for what was seen as the state's anchor TV series.

Flur S. Ence, taking the stairs back to her office, in an unknown replica of her boss's routine, remained deep in thought: an opportunity had been handed to her, of this she was vaguely aware, but she hadn't the least idea of what was going on in Vascher's head and perhaps it was just as well. When she returned to her desk she took out her binder and started to read through the script she was working on. The many tales of the revolution were known off by heart by KRAK's subjects, but looking at it with fresh eyes and connecting it to life at the moment was how Flur S. Ence imagined her new assignment. Her thoughts turned to that first meeting with Vascher where he had criticised the flags and banners and a smile crossed her face. He had been right about that but no one else had the courage to state the obvious. Perhaps that was an idea she could develop.

PAST TELL

Past Tell could perhaps be better described as a hamlet rather than a village, with its leaning cluster of lop-sided, paint-peeled, wooden houses crowded in at the four corners of the crossroads like impoverished penitents bowed in prayer.

Any visit by Dim Son brought with it convergent waves of nervous anticipation and nervous expectancy, but the sorely needed revenue that came with Dim Son's entourage was always welcome. Like the proverbial donkey, Dim Son was big when he was out, bestowing lashings of moolah for services rendered during his stay. At the same time his fearsome reputation and the rumours which reached this remote outpost had the locals on edge throughout his stay and there was always a collective sigh of relief when the helicopters spluttered back to the Ritz.

Their fears were unfounded however, as Hay Bama's presence, and Dim Son's connection to her, ensured that - despot though he was – there was no reason to interfere with the sleepy domicile. He could kill on a whim (or rather, have someone else do it for him) but he knew when to bare his teeth and when to merely show his presence. And the region around the Cream Sea did well out of it; in discreet ways getting more than its fair share of commercial contracts with the central power.

Hay Bama's modest chalet was secreted in a small copse a little farther along the expansive lake in the direction of the dominant Blue Mountains peaks, snow-covered in all seasons. She accepted the visits with equanimity; she was neither excited nor indifferent to them. She had selected Past Tell for her retirement, having gone from Daddy Kühl's dominion several years before he succumbed to liver disease, and had not even attended his funeral even though she had served him in varying capacities for over 40 years. There was no going back for Hay Bama; her successful lobbying of Daddy Kühl for an early retirement when Dim Son was old enough, ensured a smooth exit from the Ritz Corral; being on friendly terms with Madame Shoo had also helped. Her one and only obligation was to provide Dim Son with whatever services he required on a set number of occasions each year.

Dim Son's visits were moments when Hay Bama looked back and asked herself what had motivated her to get away from the Ritz. She hardly knew the answer at the time; just an inkling that urged her to extricate herself from the dysfunctional and claustrophobic life there. Only after she had made the move and was settled in Past Tell did Hay Bama feel the slow evaporation of stress and the daily existential anxiety. The Ritz Corral was a gilded cage on a massive scale, insulated from the basic layers of life and difficult to leave, but she decided that she wanted to live before she died.

He was coming. She could feel it. While there was no defined calendar date set for his visits Hay Bama could forecast their imminence. Dim Son, that unfortunate son, now more unfortunate than ever.

UP, UP AND AWAY

Preparations were well underway for the trip to Hay Bama's retreat. Madame Shoo, with her ever-present clipboard, crossed off tasks and supervised every aspect of the logistics, even ensuring that Dim Son's teddy bear was not forgotten. Whenever he travelled, it was in the middle of the night, and for no known reason. Most assumed it to be some superstition, or, less likely, security related, unaware that it was the avoidance of insomnia.

Dim Son was like a child before Christmas, eagerly anticipating the treat in store. Without fail, visits to Past Tell lightened the mood that lasted well after the encounter with Hay Bama, so that it was not only a pleasure for himself but for all those in his close proximity.

Finally they were on their way. The helicopter, a creaky old Russian model, solid as a Zetor, had been requisitioned from the mountain battalion and would ferry Dim Son and his entourage, with an escort of smaller attack helicopters to escort them on their way to the Blue Mountains.

Madame Shoo was belted in on one side of the helicopter's interior, while Dim Son was stretched out, in a water bed secured to the floor of the helicopter, reading one of his glossy magazines. He had a nosebag of Jelly Babies around his neck and occasionally he delved in and vacuumed them into his mouth by the dozen, occasionally casting fiery glances at the call girls at the far end of the helicopter.

The noise of the disappearing convoy – and the subsequent wildfire of rumour – almost influenced the local climate, as the inhabitants breathed out a collective sigh which shook the red and yellow flags and standards dotted around the leviathan Ritz.

They flew north, passing over the ascending slopes, in the direction of the peaks visible from Dim Son's residence at the Ritz. Conversation was useless; it wouldn't do to shout at Dim Son so Madame Shoo passed the time flipping through her pages of notes, ensuring that every item, however small, was ticked off. As she did so she glanced at the supplies stacked up in the middle of the wide-bellied helicopter, nodding in pleasure and confirmed to herself that her list was complete.

Dim Son tired of his magazines and threw them to one

side and tried to doze off, wrapped in his expensive fur-lined leather overcoat and matching cap. It might have been cold in the unheated helicopter but Dim Son wasn't going to feel it.

When the helicopter reached the far side of the lake it banked right and began the slow noisy descent to the chalked out landing site in the middle of a wide expanse of tundra between the lake and Past Tell. After it landed the smaller helicopters circled the area and scouted around before turning away. The ground was already crowded with the temporary military encampment and groups of soldiers were busy erecting tents. Pack animals and a number of high-wheeled jeeps ferried diverse consignments around the large plateau.

A white horse, shying at the noise from the machines and sporting a colourful embroidered blanket underneath its saddle, was brought forward by a shaven-headed youth for Dim Son's use. A less impressive dun coloured horse was made available for Madame Shoo. Everyone else walked, including the girls, who were along for the hunting expedition, while the security detachment remained at a discreet distance from the travelling party.

OPPORTUNITY KNOCKS

According to the rumours, and they are rarely inaccurate, Dim Son is out of town. One could even tell by the helium atmosphere around the place that a burden – in more ways than one -had been temporarily lifted. Speaking for myself, I was feeling pretty grounded; all thanks to my short interview with Flur S. Ence. Couldn't have gone any better really. Wirklich ausgezeichnet. I was especially pleased with my proposal that we work in small teams, opening up my two-pronged move to manage the tricky business of re-assigning the Spion. The realisation that I was making progress was a moment to savour I can tell you, and I was so proud of it that I promised myself a visit down to Slag City, being cognisant of the opportunity that Dim Son's departure brought with it.

The capital was less than twenty kilometres away and I

could be down and back while his fleshiness was cavorting up there in the hills. It had been far too long since I was outside these *verdammte* walls, and that brief epiphany on the roof had given me a taste for more; a sniff of the less rarefied life once again.

It was one hell of a garbage heap down there, but you sure could let loose with no need to watch your Ps and Qs. The crowded pavements, the twisting alleys, people surviving as best they could, the very smells; all of it had the same effect on me as a visit to the countryside had on others. Just give me a dark shebeen and a bunch of losers and I'm as right as rain again.

But first I had to finish off what I had started; I needed to get this rejigged team arrangement going as soon as possible and have everybody busy before I took off for my little break. That would also allow time for Klusch to cool his heels before he encountered me again. The moment was now; with Dim Son absent, there was also little likelihood that Madame Shoo would harass me for an audience - or a progress update, as she prefers to call it, if you please.

So, I set matters in motion, knowing that I could be downtown before evening.

'Flur?' emboldened as I was on the telephone, I dared use her first name.

'Yes?' I could hear the hesitation in her voice.

'Is it permissible to call you Flur?'

There was silence at the other end of the phone. I completely understood her dilemma.

'Only in private conversations,' I added, eager to help her out.

'Whatever you wish,' came the reply, 'whatever you think is appropriate.'

I should add here that friendships between supervisors and those who reported to them, though not common, were tolerated and the formal rules could then be relaxed somewhat.

'Thank you Flur, there is no need for you to reciprocate the greeting.'

'Thank you.'

That taken care of, I proceeded to outline the real reason for my call, injected a tone of slight urgency into my voice and, in a casual way, regularly used her first name, hoping that it would create a bond between us and, of course it would put a bit more pressure on the young woman. Unfortunate, but there you are. Needs must, omelettes and breaking eggs etc.

'I've got to research some shooting locations down in Slag and I would appreciate if you can get the teams up to speed on the new setup. Do you think that is possible Flur?'

I got a hesitant, low key affirmation - I could well imagine her reluctance. By the end of our talk however I had arranged for her to convene a meeting – on my behalf - with Klusch, where she would outline the arrangements going forward, to wit, that henceforth Klusch supervised the admin and editing groups, while Flur S. Ence worked with me as co-creator. Very nice of me, giving her the tricky job of letting him know that he was being side-lined. I could have done it myself, that I grant you, but to my way of thinking, getting Flur S. Ence to carry it out would solidify her commitment. He won't like it, oh, he won't like it one little bit.

No point, as I have said here before, of hiding my light under a bushel. I had to chuckle quietly to myself as I put the phone down, thinking of how anxious I had been back then before Dim Son's visit was announced and how splendidly things had worked out since. Modesty forbids me from clapping myself too hard on the back but credit where credit is due nevertheless.

SECONDS OUT

Dim Son was relaxed and at the same time eager as he rocked gently in the saddle. The trek across the fields was longer than the helicopter journey and traversed sheep and goat paths through the progressively rising terrain that led to Hay Bama's house. Even those so-called paths vanished as they got nearer and they had to make the rest of the way up through ferns and heather, then skirt steep and dangerous rocks and boulders and here the shaven-headed youth came into his own as he steered Dim Son's impressive mount quietly through a maze of impediments.

About 50 meters or so from the chalet Dim Son was hauled down from the horse and continued alone, walking parallel to Hay Bama's vegetable garden. His excitement built and he congratulated himself for making the trip as he approached the back door of the house. He was about to meet the person who had changed his nappy and been the nearest thing to a mother he had while growing up in Daddy Kühl's fortress.

The door was ajar and Dim Son pulled it open with a hanging leather strap that was unfastened except during night time hours. It took him a few seconds to accustom his eyes to the dim interior; weak daylight coming from a small window on the wall left of the door. The furnishings were dark and he could make out the shapes of weighty wooden objects that took on the colour of redwood in the flicker of light coming from an open fire. On the table nearest him sat a fat, lob-sided stuttering candle, its one side wax-enveloped in the shape of a frozen waterfall.

The first blow knocked him clean over. He had not seen where she had waited, for all the world just another piece of static furniture or an inanimate statue. This big woman, who must have been over 60 years of age, had the movements of an athlete and her plunging chop between his shoulder blades had sent him staggering. He banged full force into the heavy table and dropped like a felled elephant to the floor. He could hear objects falling and felt hot wax on his face. Immediately another blow came in, this time a fully-fledged kick to the solar plexus. He groaned and a trickle of vomit passed from his mouth.

Hay Bama, her long unkempt grey hair flying about her face and upper body - in other circumstances she could have passed as a bag lady - grabbed him by the lapels of his expensive coat and whacked his head back down on the wooden floor before rolling him on his side and taking careful aim kicked him repeatedly and as hard as she could on his exposed rump. She then pulled him up by the hair and shook his head from side to side before giving it one final hard whack on the floor's surface. She stopped, caught her breath, listened for a minute and, hearing no sounds, readjusted her long raincoat about her person, and sat down.

Some 20 minutes later Dim Son was on his feet and Hay Bama picked up a mallet and struck the large gong on the mantlepiece and took a seat in front of the open fire. Two of his helpers came running and collected him by the door he had entered earlier. He made his assisted way silently away from the house and paused briefly to take in the wild landscape and the expanse of water down below. He winced with pain and his face showed bruising, but it also housed an ecstatic gleam as he made his unsteady way past the cabbages and cucumbers. As he continued his descent he caught sight of Madame Shoo, leaning against a tree, ticking items in her clipboard and remembered he had something to ask her.

BLUFFER'S LUCK

Strictly speaking, foreigners like myself were not really allowed on the premises of the Ritz at all; that stipulation even applied to those with diplomatic accreditation. Trust is good, control is better, as someone once said.

After things started to fall apart back home I ended up here. It was an interesting episode and suffice it to say, Daddy Kühl had more than a bit part in how it came about. Yes, in the very early days I was holed up in what could euphemistically be called the diplomatic quarter; a dull outer suburb, which existed in a microclimate of hoary fog. This was where foreigners and undesirables were housed; a location where they could easily be observed by the hordes of secret service agents who hung around the place. The local saying, 'whatever you say, say nothing,' was truer than true. An innocent comment at the supermarket could gather legs and someone finished up in the basement of the Ritz – the only time they're going to get in there. Unfortunately, it's also a one-way ticket. I'm not exaggerating my friend - I've seen it happen. The foreigners were usually luckier and ended up with a mere expulsion unless they had been particularly stupid.

In those days – *I must go to the barber when I'm down there, the walrus needs a trim* – nothing of note happened in my world and I was still nursing the wounds of my unfortunate transfer to KRAK. I played the game, went along to exhibitions, showed my face, gave the same speech over and over, usually prefaced with the same old one liner – *thank you for that warm hand, said the cow to the farmer on a frosty morning* - until one day I received a quasi-invitation to a theatre rehearsal in the city centre; my ethnicity and knowledge being kindly requested as a consultant to the troupe. And the reason, as I would later find out, was that Daddy Kühl himself would be in attendance.

It was a Brecht piece, well known to me and I was indeed curious as to how they would interpret it over here. To cut to the chase, they were making a donkey's hames of it. Not a clue. For a start the translation was abysmal – by this time I had a more than reasonable fluency in the local language – but the direction, and the acting in particular, was not even at the standard of bad amateur. In my modest way I proffered diplomatic comments, and confined myself to improvements that could be made to the translation.

One of the team, the producer no less, took me to one side.

'*Scheiße, absolut scheiße,*' he hissed, 'the translation is done by those cretins up at the Ritz and they insist that we only use their director and actors, all of them from the *Gewerkschaft der Arschlecker*.' I had not only met someone unafraid to speak his mind, but a fellow ex-pat, well almost a compatriot – he was a *Wessie*. We spoke quietly among ourselves and I became more forthcoming as to my real thoughts on the production.

Sepp Seife, for it was he, had appeared out of the woodwork and I had a soul brother at last. It had taken a year in the godforsaken dump, a year that almost made me pine for my previous assignment as a liaison between my old regime and the revolutionary movement on the *Grüne Insel*. I had to fuck that up, didn't I? And boy did they let me know that I had fucked up. Sorry, another story…where was I? Ah yes, my good old *Kumpel*, Sepp. We took to each other with the enthusiasm of long lost friends. Sepp was a bit of a *Lebenskünstler* and had finished up in KRAK through mischief or the mad headedness of youth, most likely a combination of the two.

The bane of his life back then was the setup of incompetents and cronies he had to deal with – 100 percent selected according to the purity of belief in the system - and he would go off into long diatribes about the cultural committee at the drop of a hat, and before I knew where I was he had installed me as the director of Mother Courage, an honour to be sure.

To be strictly accurate here, I just may have given him a polished, if not to say a somewhat fictional summary of my *Lebenslauf*. How as ever, Sepp and myself rolled up our sleeves and got together a near enough first rate production of the play. And Sepp, although I didn't know about this at the time - I swear! - had a line into Daddy Kühl.

Two events then occurred: one, I was allowed to move into an apartment near the centre of the city because of the theatre work; a downgrade to be sure on material comfort but a Great Leap Forward in terms of culture and associated nightlife. Damn it, life was almost normal in that part of town; there were bars and clubs, cheap restaurants and cinemas, not to mention our own theatre.

Two, I was to meet Daddy Kühl, and mightily impressed he was at our gala opening night! It must have been a revelation, and a relief for him to be treated to a professional-level performance. My, oh my, I did have it back then; took no prisoners and hit on a perfect combination - my talent and the work rate of others.

Here I should say, on meeting the man himself, although

overawed and as nervous as Flur S. Ence was in my office just recently, I did somehow manage to maintain my *sangfroid*, no doubt helped by being confronted by this leprechaun of a man with the flowing hair and loud cravat.

'Ah ha, the real thing my comrade - most excellent indeed,' he enthused, taking my hand in both of his as he stepped back slightly and looked up at me and scrutinised every twitch on my face. Now I am not a tall man but I felt like an ungainly giant in his close proximity. I bowed graciously and also moved back a tad in a polite effort to further reduce the differential in heights.

'Your Brecht never fails to impress - "war is like love, it finds its way" ha-ha, but seriously, I must congratulate you on the production here this evening; it is rarely our cultural guests show initiative of this sort.'

I was quick to ring the praises of Sepp, knowing of course that it would do myself no disservice. Daddy Kühl continued to quiz me on my background and, having satisfied himself with my embellished history and, mutual elevations long forgotten, leaned in close, 'I think you need a larger audience Mr Vascher.'

Well now, there isn't a stage large enough that could daunt Yours Truly, at least in theory and to cut a rather convoluted story short – and it was always somewhat convoluted with DK. Soon afterwards I finished up with the gig known as the

Dim Dynasty Tales.

All these memories stirred in the shale of my mental alluvium. *'Think back Vascher, think back and then think again.'* For the present though I had to get my mind around my main task of the evening. It's not that easy you know – getting from the Ritz to downtown. *Bestechung* was your only man. I checked my wallet and got myself shaved, remembering as I looked in the mirror to head to the barbers first thing.

AFTERS

The group with Dim Son, those near and far, returned by the steep path to where camp had been set up. Madame Shoo gave an order to the youngster leading Dim Son's animal and he turned to his left, leading the horse and its cargo in the direction of a large tent at the far end of the plateau. After he had been taken from the horse, Madame Shoo waited until he had composed himself and led the way slowly to the tent entrance.

Dim Son, accompanied by a small detachment of soldiers, followed slowly, limping slightly and his patent leather shoes squelching in the wet ground. This did not go unnoticed by Madame Shoo and she could be seen making notes on her clipboard. She walked marginally ahead of Dim Son and waited until he came up and pulled back the tent's large flap which obscured the interior. Dim Son, whose eyes still retained their renewed lustre, was about to step inside when he remembered what it was he wanted.

'When are we having our first showing?' he asked.

The question baffled Madame Shoo and she looked blankly at him, for a brief moment afraid that she had forgotten to arrange some key entertainment for the outing.

'I beg your pardon, Your Excellency?'

'The show, the damn show, the Vascher thing,' he spluttered as he scraped some remaining wax from his face.

'Oh *that*,' Madame Shoo recovered, 'I'll check with Vascher as soon as I'm back at the Ritz Corral.'

'You do that. You *make sure* you do that,' and there was no mistaken the menace in his voice. Madame Shoo had not been the recipient of this tone before and it disturbed her.

'I'll go back on one of the support helicopters and deal with it immediately,' she countered and it seemed to have the requisite effect as Dim Son entered the tent to be engulfed by a gaggle of goodtime girls within. Madame Shoo returned to the improvised helipad to wait for the helicopter which would take her back to the Ritz.

Dim Son would later 'free' his retinue of hired women and allow them to wander through the countryside around Cream Sea, sometime later setting out with a hunting party to track them down. Dim Son liked the chase, although if truth be known, he wouldn't have trapped a single girl if he had to heave his bulk through the countryside on his own. On horseback and with a retinue of pointers and beaters to locate prey, he was handed his quarry on a plate on which he gorged himself.

HITTING THE TOWN

I hung around Pillar 8, sussed out the potentials and picked up a lift was from one of the vegetable delivery trucks. You don't just go with anyone you know – that might be painful, and Klusch isn't the only Spitzel around here. My cover was facilitated by a permanent all-areas card which, in contrast to my office space, had not been taken away – most likely due to bureaucratic lag. The card permitted day trips outside the Ritz but would not cover overnight stays, but my driver didn't need, or want, to know anything about that. Whoever accepted knew he was taking a relatively low risk for about 10 times the regular fare.

The overnight pass would be very handy but I couldn't very well apply for it as that would very likely have thrown up the information that I had retained my all-areas ID, putting that at risk too; anyway you couldn't get an overnight in less than a week, and that was if there were no supplementaries, and as everyone who lived in KRAK knew, there were always supplementaries.

My van wasn't going anywhere near the 'theatre district' and when I told the driver where I was headed he got nervous, but I was able to quell his anxiety by letting him know I was the director of the DDT TV show and was here to check out location settings. I didn't even have to lie, not really.

He dropped me off near the remnants of the old city walls – grassed over mounds of fitful grass, earth and protruding rock. Then, after my promised and pleasurable facial trim, I had but a short walk to The Rising Sun – how apt in retrospect – the old *Kneipe* of fond memory. If Sepp weren't about, the cliental or bar staff would surely know where to find him. I had a spring in my step and hadn't realised just how much the Ritz gets into your very bones and cauterises you from the greater reality of life.

It had been raining earlier and the pavements glistened from the hanging lamps and the sparse evening vehicular traffic. Even though it was relatively early, at this time of year there were shadows and darkness in the nooks and crannies of the laneways that snaked down from the main artery towards the port. Hoarse voices could be heard shouting, ordering and complaining as I walked along – all somewhat familiar, as if I had never left the area. The Rising Sun was on the corner of a spartan open square, its pocked sign rustling in the breeze. It had seen better days but I looked on it like a long lost friend and it was with something approaching joy and anticipation that I entered.

I pushed past the swing doors, lifted the latch on the internal door and looked at a scene that had not altered a great deal since the times we used to haunt it before and after rehearsals. It was also our *Stammtisch* on non-performance nights; you could even say I was there most evenings –with Sepp and His Merrie Men. What days my friend! Oh we were full of it; saw ourselves as the *avant-garde*, and not lacking in arrogance either – if you can believe that! Drizzle on some self-importance if you so wish. Sepp and myself were trophies of a type – foreigners – the cool of the *übercool*. And when my break came with the coolest Daddy of them all, well, need I say more? Talk about farting in silk.

The bar was quiet, soft conversations breaking gently over the silence and that familiar clammy atmosphere I remembered from the past. It was a bit early for a crowd and I didn't recognise a sinner, not even the bar staff, and I must admit I felt a frisson of hostility from those inside as I walked towards the counter – the place had never been like this in our day, even if I was a stranger and some curiosity was to be expected. Back in the day we welcomed newcomers, indeed we welcomed anyone who brought something to the party; not anymore it would seem.

'Does Sepp Seife still drink here?' I asked the young barman behind the counter.

'Do you know him?' he replied, in a sullen tone.

'Oh yes,' I said, twirling my refreshed moustaches, 'we were drinking buddies in the old days.'

'I haven't seen you in here before.'

Well, that was reasonable enough, so I asked another question: 'How long have you been working here?'

'Five years.'

I couldn't hide my astonishment and looked around.

'Five years,' I gasped, 'it can't have been that long…'

The barman's look took on a more conciliatory attitude, 'yes, lots of changes since Daddy Kühl's departure.'

I leant back against a high stool, the pillar behind it preventing it from moving and looked again at the barman. I could see that he was taking in my reaction.

'Yes, the days of Daddy Kühl are gone,' I said, and I couldn't fail to notice the tone of regret in my voice.

'Sepp still drinks here,' the barman's friendlier voice pulled me out of my reverie, 'I can probably reach him for you if you wish; he lives in the neighbourhood, although we don't see that much of him these days.'

The change in the barman's demeanour caught me on the hop and despite some suspicions I gave my name (modestly omitting the Chief bit).

'Okay, I'll get a message to him,' he confirmed, and asked me if I wanted a drink.

'A double Chivas,' I replied.

He laughed loudly. 'It *is* a while since you've been here alright,' he said, struggling to contain his mirth, 'the Chivas ran out before Daddy Kühl did.'

It was my turn to look astonished once again. No Chivas! What in earth was the world coming to?

'Slag Brau is all we've got I'm afraid.'

'Okay, I'll try one of them,' I responded, as my pleasant humour took a downhill turn.

AWOL

Madame Shoo, somewhat flustered, returned to the Ritz while Dim Son and his entourage remained on for the subsequent hunting expedition. She had dealt with the logistics but she would take no further part in the outing. She had made that clear to Dim Son; there was so far she was willing to go arranging his diversions, but she had no intention of staying huddled up in a helicopter while Dim Son played Cowboys & Indians with an extended troupe of gym girls brought along for his entertainment.

She had more than enough on her mind; for starters she needed to contact Chief Boddle Vascher and ascertain if the TV serial was tracking according to plan; she needed to impart to him Dim Son's wish for a pilot program to be made available ASAP. That wasn't going to go down too well but there you had it; Vascher should understand a decree from Dim Son as well as most.

To her consternation, Vascher couldn't be located when she tried to arrange a meeting and word came back that he was not in the building. Where was he then? He was in the city. In the city? Well! Being Madame Shoo, she queried the Exit Pass Database and saw that Vascher's pass hadn't scanned his presence in the Ritz since earlier that afternoon. His All Areas pass was valid and there was nothing she could do about it now but wait. He had tricked her again.

Livid, she paced up and down the office venting loudly, pausing just briefly to log in and revoke his All Areas permission with immediate effect. After she cooled down she realised what it was she hated about the bag of wind who passed as a TV producer: he did as he pleased and got away with it time and again, while she dared not have a hair out of place, and on top of that her failure to turn the tables on him at the Dim Son meeting stung to the quick. 'Damn that man to hell,' she screamed as she threw her clipboard across the floor and went and collected it immediately.

TEMPUS FUGIT

I concluded my brief conversation with the young barman and took the flat beer and sat at a small table by the windowless wall opposite the entrance. A feeling that I had made a big mistake by coming down here began to disconcert me; coming to The Rising Sun came across as a careless impulse. Sepp Seife and His Merrie Men indeed!

A type of panic overcame me and even though I had come specifically to meet Sepp, all of a sudden I was fearful of the encounter. But I held my ground and fought back my baser instincts. Boddle Vascher might be going down but he was not going to run out on himself.

I drank the beer, curling up my nose to lessen its interesting aroma and recovered my equilibrium. There was no sign of Sepp and I went up for another drink. The barman served me as if he had never seen me before and I quietly returned to my seat. My second glass was half empty – the stuff was well manky and of dubious strength - when Sepp walked in the door and something told me that he had me checked out before making his appearance. Sepp had changed and if I had not known he was coming I think I might not have recognised him at all.

Gaunt, unshaven, wearing a long black coat; my first impression was – believe it or not – an Angel of Death. He didn't see me straightaway in the dim interior, or pretended not to, and I watched his eyes dart around the room. He looked at the barman who nicked his head in the direction where I was seated. Sepp approached cautiously, as if he was stepping between hidden mines and his eyes squinted as he approached. I stood up and extended my hand, 'Sepp,' I said simply.

He took my hand mechanically, but his attention was somewhere else, as if my presence had transported him to another time.

'Boddle?' he asked.

'At your service, or should I say, one of the Merrie Men at your service.'

His mouth developed a faint smile, accentuating the many wrinkles that converged around his lips.

'It is you,' he confirmed to himself.

'A drink?' I asked, moving towards the bar.

'Yes, thank you.'

I took my glass with me and drained the remainder while I waited for the new drinks to be poured. When I returned Sepp had seated himself and was leaning against the sweaty black painted wall, looking as if he was unravelling some complicated formula.

'To old times,' I said, seating myself and raising my glass to touch his, 'and old friends.'

For several minutes we drank silently and again the thought that I never should have come here crossed my mind and, despite my outward bonhomie I was somewhat tongue-tied and unable to anchor myself in what had become a strange place; a place that hovered between the present and the past.

But eventually we did get going, propelled by yours truly - ahead of the posse as usual - trying my best to revive a relationship of yore. And it worked, despite rather than as a result of the insipid beer. Inhibitions loosened, although I must add that we did not descend into drunkenness, impossible with the strength of that boot wash, nor did we slink into maudlin sentimentality; *au contraire*, it was as if the chemistry between us had rekindled and transformed itself into the key that unlocked our shared and unshared past.

REACQUAINTANCE

Sepp and myself were sizing each other up as we talked. How had I done; how had he done? Who had been the lucky one? All that sort of baloney. Sepp knew as well as I did that it was Daddy Kühl's little dilemma that had led to my transfer to the Ritz. If that hadn't happened I wouldn't be here but most likely going through an '*Aufklärungsprozeß*' back at home.

'That program of yours has gone to the dogs,' Sepp said after his tongue had been loosened and we started to talk frankly again as friends, leaving the polite conversation of half strangers behind us.

'That, coming from you, is a shocking indictment,' I countered, agreeing with him but deciding to play the contrarian, 'it's one of the stars of the TV schedule and possibly the longest running program on television *anywhere*; even longer than The Mousetrap at this stage, I'll have you know.'

Sepp laughed.

'And The Mousetrap only ran that long because Agatha Christie decided to pull a publicity stunt by dying,' I continued.

Sepp laughed again – he knew me for the bullshitter that I am.

'You're some cookie Boddle. Not that I,' and here he got serious, '...not that I've been knocking out Brecht-like innovations in recent years.'

'I'm inclined to believe you,' I said, looking around, 'what's happened to this place?'

'Those days are gone Boddle... for us in any case.'

'You think so?'

'I know so.'

'Maybe,' I sighed, the image of a falling brick striking me as the symbol of my own downward trajectory.

'They'll come again... but not for us,' he concluded, triggering a temporary bout of philosophical pondering on my part. Sepp and myself were men of our time. Maybe we just consoled ourselves with an invented narrative to suit our present status?

I gave Sepp a brief *résumé* of the contortions required to impress Madame Shoo and Dim Son and, to my surprise, he looked interested, chuckling along as I recounted the entire slapstick routine. That greyness which I had noticed when I first saw him had evaporated and that old gleam of devilment was back in his eyes. He admitted he was impressed; even went as far to say he was ever so slightly envious of how I had turned the tables on them.

'But to be frank Sepp, I had given up; I think it was naked fear drove me back into the game.' Sepp was looking intently at me, a puzzled amusement in his glance.

'*Echt Sepp, absolute Furcht.*'

'But you're on the inside track up there Boddle.'

'Was!'

'Oh?'

'Being Daddy Kühl's mate had, shall we say, certain disadvantages after his decease. *Verstehst Du jetzt?*'

'The young buck was jealous?'

'*Ja genau.* Wants to make his own mark.'

'Hmm... that could be tricky.'

'You better believe it.'

'So you've backed yourself with one last roll of the dice, *nicht wahr?*'

'*Richtig.* You may wonder why this dread engulfed me? Well, I'll tell you. The guy is a psychopath, pure and simple. I'm no psychologist but the absence of a mother and a distant father have had an effect. Not a good one.'

'The rumours down here are of the blood curdling sort. Is it true that the young fellow has had most of his father's inner circle terminated?'

'With extreme prejudice. Practically all of them *mein*

Freund. My dread was that he was going to delve into *die Zweite Reihe!*'

'*Das glaube ich nicht.* What would be the point in that? No disrespect, but surely he doesn't see you as a danger to the new fellow?'

'I wouldn't be so sure Sepp. Like I said,' I gestured at my temple, take out a few, frighten the rest, and very soon you have a compliant crew capable of doing just about anything to survive.'

Sepp signalled the barman for another round of drinks and shook himself as if dispersing the information I had given him before letting out a long whistle.

'I suppose I should be happy down here,' he concluded to himself, 'where I can decline gracefully.'

'There's a lot to be said for that.'

'You could come back,' he chirped back, his eyes twinkling, an echo of the *Frechheit* he possessed as a young man.

'Or you could come to the Ritz,' I countered.

Even though I had my tongue firmly in cheek, I had niggled him and he jerked back in his seat, the chair making an ugly noise on the stone-flagged floor.

'Not on your life,' he spat out, 'Remember those feral cats who used to hang around the old theatre Boddle? Well, that's me. I understood your particular situation when we took separate paths back then; mine may be a bit stonier, but I'll persevere thank you very much.'

I decided to pursue the subject a little further, just for the hell of it. 'I'm not pushing it Sepp – you know what they say about examining all the alternatives in the cold light of day.'

He looked hard at me. Even though we knew each other for many years, I sometimes thought that Sepp Seife didn't know me at all – nor I him. There was a long silence and I knew that it was time to talk about what I really had on my mind.

'You could say that this visit is a type of a toe in the water exercise, having a look around here to see if I could fit in again. What do you think?'

'Do you want to fit in, is more the question.'

'I've become part of the furniture up above and despite some humiliations in recent times, it is a reasonably comfortable gig, maybe too comfortable – although I shouldn't say that for a number of reasons.'

'Maybe we are both where we want to be,' Sepp mused.

'I'll drink to that,' it was my turn to resort to levity, 'what a mess, what a wonderful mess we've made of it all Sepp, the young tyros of yesteryear.'

Having got all that off our chests, Sepp and I settled down to small talk and dug up old memories of fellow thespians and crew members from the Strolling Players era. Some had vanished into the ether, some had passed away, others were hanging around somewhere.

I was the only one to make it up to the Ritz, and the sole reason was that Daddy Kühl had summoned me on the basis of my transformative work at the city theatre. Ever aware of the power he had amassed, he had hit upon the idea of a TV series as a morale booster and a distraction for the general populace, knowing, as he did by then, that the promises of the revolution had petered out one by one.

One thing was a constant with Daddy Kühl: he never mixed down here with up above. It suited him too, and having one of his unofficial retinue at close quarters meant that the Chivas Regal parties could be enjoyed without the inconvenience of travel, security and all that goes with that. He never though, not once and with no exceptions – Sepp included – invited any others of the downtown crew up to the Ritz. After I had gone through the drawbridge, the portcullis came down and with it the downtown romps.

'Between ourselves, I mean *strictly* between us,' I whispered, 'I have entertained thoughts of getting out – I mean really getting out. Out, out, out, if you gather my meaning.'

'Why doesn't that surprise me?'

'The gilded cage may be my destiny Sepp but I have to see if I can warble my way to some meaningful form of existence outside its golden bars.'

'You haven't lost the poetic flourish I see,' Sepp said as he raised his glass and clinked mine.

Unnoticed, the barman arrived at the table, bearing two plates of cooked black pudding.

'Ah, *Blutwurst,*' I cried out as I grabbed a cocktail stick and speared one of the pocked glutinous cylinders.

'On the house,' the barman said, as he removed the empties with a flourish.

As I took in Sepp's facial features with my peripheral vision, I realised that the years, nay, decades, had evaporated and the greyness of his skin and sparse hair reminded me that he was almost an old man, and that could only mean that the same characterisation applied to myself.

'I think you know yourself Boddle, I mean why we both are where we are,' Sepp said, and it took me a few minutes to remember what he was referring to, so busy had I become lobbing back rounds of black pudding. I couldn't quite tell you the difference between the two of us, but there was something about Sepp that couldn't tolerate or bear that which had to be borne if one lived up at the Ritz. No, even though it meant slow decline and, to a certain extent, irrelevance, Sepp had decided that the place for him was in the midst of the slag heap of a city. Don't ask me whether Daddy Kühl made a proposal to him. I have no idea.

And this brought me to a conclusion about myself. When I thought about it, I could have stayed down here too. My role at the Cultural Institute would have been terminated of course, but I could have survived; the theatre had an arts grant and a personal stipend, small to be sure, but enough to tie me over in modest circumstances.

Why had Daddy Kühl made his offer? It wouldn't surprise me in the least if he had just wanted a convenient drinking buddy and conversationalist close at hand. He wasn't getting any younger and the trip down here must have become a bit of a pain as time went on. There we had it, insight and enlightenment as I sat drinking tepid beer and scoffing black pudding.

'What are you really doing down here?' Sepp asked, taking me off guard.

'Good one Sepp, good one,'

And it was. I needed time to take that question in. I could blather a meaningless reply and leave it at that, but I was talking to Sepp, someone who knew me and was not just shooting the breeze. I felt a pensiveness come over me as the evening turned into one of reflection and cold reckoning. What was I up to and why was I down here for the first time in years?

I didn't have an answer and I was too proud to admit that I was flailing about like a stranded fish, gasping for something to set me in motion again. Perhaps, as I had suspected, it was a mistake on my part, coming back to the scene of an earlier existence, trying to rake something up from the shrivelled ashes of incinerated memories.

'One last look Sepp? Don't ask me! It could be a hundred different ideas that brought me down here – it's a bit like burying the dead.'

'Have you run out of road Boddle?' And there the conversation came to a halt.

Instead of quelling our appetites, the black pudding had only whetted them more. We stumbled out of the bar and wandered over to the Quays where we ate from a menu that hadn't changed since my day. Not that it mattered that much, we just required ballast to keep us going that bit longer, and 'a bit longer' became a lot longer, and we continued late into the night. I abandoned any indistinct plan I had of getting back to the Ritz, something I really shouldn't have done; there would be consequences, but my rampant bravado decided that I would negotiate my way back inside in the morning and be damned with the fallout.

I finished up sleeping in Sepp's sofa and awoke with a nasty headache and the realisation that I had a meeting with Flur S. Ence before noon. My plan had been to extend the meeting and invite her to lunch in the galley where we could 'deepen' the relationship. Sepp was asleep when I arose and I didn't wake him. I blundered about a bit, got dressed, stuffed a few pieces of bread in my mouth, gulped down a beaker of water and headed over to the municipal market for a lift back up the hills.

MADAME AMISS

She couldn't locate Chief Boddle Vascher, and she was unable to determine his whereabouts from the various emissaries and agents she had sent searching through the Ritz. She knew he had gone to the city the previous day, but now it was clear that he had stayed out overnight, a serious offence for which he would pay. To lance her anger she decided to go hunting herself, distasteful and demeaning as she found it, and off she went, down to the lower decks and stormed through drab corridors she rarely had reason to traverse.

Upon entering Vascher's office, she closed the door and rooted around inside while her personal bodyguard remained on guard in the corridor. She sifted through the unholy mess looking for any clue as to what he might be up to. She experienced the untidiness and chaos of the office as almost offensive; piles of scribbled notes, scripts, books, papers and magazines, stacked or strewn; unfinished cups of coffee; a stale smell from overflowing ashtrays, remnants of food. Did the cleaners ever come around here, she wondered, forgetting that at this level people had to clean up for themselves.

Notwithstanding a thorough search she found nothing of interest and speculated when was the last time Vascher had as much as reviewed or read the material scattered around the place. She stood there for several minutes, a beacon of order and tidiness in the midst of the displaced matter, her clipboard hugged to her chest.

While contemplating a suitable retaliation for the vexatious producer, a knock came from the door and her sentry poked his head in, 'Visitor for Chief Boddle Vascher.' Madame Shoo went to the door and saw a vaguely familiar face, although she couldn't place it immediately.

'Yes,' she asked, putting on her most imperious voice.

'I'm here to see Chief Boddle Vascher,' Flur S. Ence answered, and as soon as she did so, Madame Shoo remembered the young woman who had sat quietly at the table during Vascher's presentation.

'Ah, Miss Flur S. Ence from the presentation. He's not here I'm afraid. Do *you* have any idea where he might be?'

A puzzled look spread across the young woman's face, already uncomfortable in front of the high-ranking personage.

'Why don't you step in here?' Madame Shoo said, stepping to one side. The young woman moved mechanically into the room and Madame Shoo closed the door for a second time. Both women remained standing.

'I've been looking for Chief Boddle Vascher since last evening. He has gone ashore and apparently has not returned. Did he by any chance give you any indication that he intended to flee?'

That last word frightened Flur S. Ence, bringing up, as it did, images of a fugitive on the run and she sensed a vibration of real danger that emanated from Madame Shoo.

'We are working on the new script and I'm here for a follow-up meeting on the overall approach and the division of resources. I didn't know Chief Boddle Vascher was away.'

Madame Shoo motioned Flur S. Ence to sit and pursued her interrogation – for that is what it was – for several minutes more until she satisfied herself that the young woman knew nothing of a possible abscondment. She would deal with Vascher's breaking of the curfew later. In the meantime her attention was taken by this person in front of her; there was something in the way Flur S. Ence conducted herself that impressed her and she changed the subject completely and began to probe the young woman about the new series.

'So, tell me, how have you finished up in the Ritz Corral?

You are a city girl I can tell from your accent.'

'Yes, my parents live in Slag City. I was chosen for the Academy as a young girl.'

'Ah, we have a scholarship girl. How nice. Well, now we have something in common – I arrived here in the same circumstances... many years ago now,' she concluded with a little exhalation of breath.

The incongruity of Flur S. Ence's punctiliousness in manner did not escape her; she had a minimalism that suggested tidiness and order, something close to Madame Shoo's heart and in sharp contrast to the mess in Vascher's office. As the conversation relaxed – steered by Madame Shoo's manipulative questions - a clearer picture of this young intern emerged in her mind and the creative store of Flur S. Ence's expressed ideas impressed her. What struck her even more was the self-control and calmness of the young woman; she knew what she was about, she didn't try to impress, she listened, she considered before answering questions and, above all, she – although possibly unaware of it herself – exuded a self-contained inner authority and dependability.

Madame Shoo had been of the opinion – even in Daddy Kühl's day – that Vascher was an out and out bluffer and had prospered as a kind of court jester for the former ruler. The thought that Vascher's days could be made redundant by this young lady sitting primly amidst the detritus of the office crossed her mind.

Should it be allowed to shine its light on a bigger stage, then the old windbag might well be going down a few more floors. This was an option for the future, too early to bring into play just yet; however, one day the cards were sure to fall differently. The women were concluding their conversation, having moved on to chit-chat when the door burst open.

SNIFFING DANGER

'Verdammter Wächter, was macht der hier?' I shouted as I barged through to my office. A sentry before my door if you don't mind. So eine Frechheit. In my still somewhat inebriated state I didn't take in the possible seriousness of it and I had breezed past him to see of all people, Madame Shoo in conversation with my rising star, in my office! In a warm tête-à-tête I might add. Madame Shoo looked across at me, a guilty look mingled with an exasperated tightness of body and before I could quite get my bearings she slipped past me, issuing some edict or other about yet another meeting as she left. What was going on?

I waited a few minutes and went to the door and peeped out into an empty corridor. 'Gone, both of them' I muttered, '*ach, mein Kopf!*'

At first it was as if I had forgotten that Flur S. Ence was in the room but when she asked if she could go, I jerked my head and almost shouted, '*Nein, nein,* no, no,' and apologising for my tone, whispered, 'what did she want?'

'I don't know, she was already here when I came up for the meeting.'

My eyes darted around the office and then realised that it was impossible to know if anyone had been going through my documents and cursed under my breath.

'What did you talk about?' my gaze swung back to Flur S. Ence.

'Oh, the series… and she wanted to know things about me.'

Oh she did now, did she, I thought. I bet she did.

'Well, never mind all that,' I said, my poise recovered, 'could I just ask you one tiny, tiny little favour?' And without waiting for an answer, I continued, 'the success of any enterprise, especially one of this magnitude, requires absolute loyalty on the part of the team. Do you understand me?'

Without further ado, I set to extracting what information I could from Flur S. Ence. Now, you must be careful with that sort of thing; ask the wrong questions and you give away too much about your own fears and hopes, ask too little and you've wasted your time – it's always a balancing act.

What I gleaned did not, at first reading, signal any danger

to my good self. They had come together by pure coincidence; indeed Flur S. Ence was supposed to be in my office for our meeting at this time. I put the episode aside, little suspecting at the time that the kernel of an abominable plan had begun to form in Madame Shoo's mind. Flur S. Ence knew nothing of this and it was up to me to shelter and protect her, while doing myself no disservice of course, if you get my drift, nod, nod, wink, wink.

I was still in recovery mode from the blow-out with Sepp, but bit by bit I rediscovered my old zip and started to pace up and down the tiny room, throwing out ideas and scenarios for the new production. Flur S. Ence diligently made notes in her little lined notebook – standard issue, cheap, greyish paper, faded lines – while I rambled on in an ever expanding manner, finding it rather cute the way she held her notebook in mid-air as she wrote.

'Do you think you could put all that together in a coherent draft' I asked, 'I know it's complicated and multi-layered – and a little random - but I think you have understood, no?' I concluded with a smile that signalled the conclusion of my input for the time being. Flur S. Ence looked at me and if she wondered what in the hell was going on, she did a very good job at disguising it.

'Yes Chief,' she replied, 'shall I expand the dialogue or is your preference to leave it at the conceptual phase for the moment?'

'Hmm, yes, conceptual did you say?... spot on Flur... the conceptual phase, quite right. *Verdammt klug, die junge Frau...* I caught myself on, thankful that she didn't know the language, although you'd never know with her, so damned clever, 'oh, by the way could you get a progress report for Madame Shoo's meeting. She did say tomorrow, didn't she?'

ARE WE THERE YET?

The happy coincidence of meeting Flur S. Ence and the slipperiness of Vascher juxtaposed in Madame Shoo's thoughts, the one giving her an idea and the other the cause of concern. It was easy, too easy, to underestimate Vascher, that she already knew from the Daddy Kühl era. Not only that, but she could also attest to his most recent renaissance – if that were the word – and how he had turned the tables at the Dim Son meeting, something she had foreseen as the penultimate step to his extinction, career-wise at least, but there he had slipped the noose once again.

Flur S. Ence would suit her better; she embodied all that was praiseworthy in Madame Shoo's book. While she was not contemplating a legacy just yet, now and then she played around with long-term succession scenarios. She examined her own motivation and found it difficult to look beyond efficiency and organisational ability. Was there anything else there? She didn't know. She was well aware that she stood at the very centre of the machine, had served it faithfully going on two generations, never once came into the crossfires of purges or heaves, simply did her master's bidding and left the rest to work itself out. And that had stood to her, no one could deny that.

'Slowly, slowly, catchee monkey,' she muttered as a knock came to the door and her guard informed her that Dim Son had returned and had urgently requested her presence. 'When is it not urgent?' Madame Shoo groaned and made her way over to the state departments.

Dim Son still had the bee in his bonnet and wanted to know if the new series was ready yet and when told that it was not, wanted to know what was holding it up. He looked a bit washed up after his purge at the hands of Hay Bama and the follow-on 'hunting' expedition. It took all her powers of persuasion to explain the time needed to have a production of this sort completed. Even she knew that a serviceable version of the script, let alone the first rushes for the series itself, could not have been produced in the interval since approval, but logic never entered into it.

Dealing with Dim Son in this mood was like having to deal with a child in a sweet shop where one made promises of something better down the line. And who could be better qualified for that task, she thought, than Vascher - purveyor of smokes and daggers – and she decided to let him manage Dim Son, after all he was probably still gloating on the marvellous show he put on last time. 'Let's see how his grand scheme works now,' and a smile almost escaped onto her face.

CHIEF GLOATER

Things are going swimmingly ever since my return from the impromptu trip down memory lane with Sepp. You do need that sort of thing occasionally I think, an opportunity to let off frustrations and blow fresh air through the grey matter. I am grateful to Sepp for that; believe me I needed it. At the same time I have learned a lesson – there is no going back and, while not quite possessing the finality of death, the past is a closed door which cannot be re-opened; only be re-imagined. That thought sobers me up, sweeps away my nostalgia and brings me smack into the present.

I can't really explain it to you properly in words, but a bolt of iron has entered me, *echt Eisen,* and if I happen to be on a downhill train then I am going to drive to the limit, fill it to the gills, burn it to a cinder; I am not going to be stopped, by hell or Dim Son. Speaking of which, I have to deal with this request for yet another meeting – *bitte!* – from herself, some sort of progress report I am to understand. Progress my arse. Better to take Flur S. Ence along though, I reckon; she can take them through the bits and bytes of whatever progress they are looking for – that stuff bores me utterly.

Bring it on, let us get to the stub of the matter. You know - this might give you a titter - I've just realised that all of this Dim Son wants this and Madame Shoo gets that; all of that plays right into my hands - more than that actually, it could positively drive my agenda, and the beauty of it all is that I didn't really have to do anything; just turn up basically – brush some honey around their mouths and let the rest flow from there. *Mensch!*

JITTERY POKER

Flur S. Ence knew she was getting caught up in something; she didn't know what it was but she was sure that whatever it was, she needed to be careful. She felt too inexperienced to understand, let alone participate in the office politics of the TV studio, having been recently plucked from the obscure Peoples' Scientific Journal, where she transformed technical articles into layman's language. The Scientific was sacrificed, along with much of the non-essential propaganda outlets when budgets tightened.

Staff were relocated to what were deemed essential sections by raffle ticket, and so, quite accidently she had landed in Vascher's domain. This was a whole new ball game for Flur S. Ence, but being a fast learner, within a few months she had mastered not just the technical television programming requirements, but had also shown a clear understanding of what it took to get episodes from a rough and ready idea onto screen.

She sat quietly, two large reams of paper in front of her on the desk; on the one were headings for the creative side of the equation: approach, style, form, structure, and on the other the practical necessities: cast, locations, research, sources etc.

The meeting was not be in the Creative offices but in Dim Son's staterooms on the top deck. Could she believe such a thing? That area of the building was so remote that it almost didn't exist in her mind and she couldn't put away anxious feelings as she contemplated sitting there, afraid to breathe. What if someone asked her a difficult question, could she answer? She hoped that the Chief would take care of that.

She was eager to learn what Chief Boddle Vascher required from her at the meeting, but protocol forbade contacting him; she would have to wait for his initiative. And so she sat there, working deeper into the script as these thoughts surfaced and went on their way again.

Flur S. Ence and her colleague were wedged into a tight space with just enough elbow room to work on the shared table. She suspected that Klusch was a spy, although that was not the word she used – officially he was a Purification Overseer; someone tasked with ensuring that anything which might offend the regime didn't find its way into published scripts.

THIS MORTAL COIL

Dim Son was in the library, leafing through one of his magazines, on official censorship duty. He was somewhat exhausted in the wake of his jaunt in the Blue Mountains and, although he had thoroughly enjoyed his extended joust in trying conditions, his feeling now was tending towards the morose; the emptiness starting to well up once again. The pictures he flicked through failed to excite and he hadn't resumed his morning gym session since his return – a sure sign that he was not in the best state of mind. He was brooding and when Dim Son brooded, someone else was sure to get it in the neck.

He got up and paced around the low, heavy table, laden with books and magazines awaiting review. He returned to his bedroom and opened the drawer of the bedside table, pulled out the black book and, after pressing the door switch, went out on to the balcony when the silently sliding glass doors retracted. It was mid-morning he guessed, although in truth it was early afternoon. There was a chill in the air and Dim Son returned to the bedroom where he wrapped himself in his Onesie and turned on the balcony heaters. He lay on the recliner and looked across at the mountains. From his perch on the top deck the distance between himself and the mountains had shrunk and he felt as if he could almost reach out and touch the slopes stretching up from the invisible valley. His mind briefly returned to the 'hunt' at the other side of the mountains and he resolved to repeat the adventure later in the Spring.

'He who eats this bread and drinks this wine will live forever,' he read from the skinny pages of the densely printed text, and speculated on the bread and wine with these properties. This rumination eventually triggered thoughts on the new TV series, which had disappeared from his radar, now rushed back to him. Irritation took hold and he fumed that no one had informed him of progress; he had assumed that it must already be long past completion. A childhood of unrestricted and immediate indulgence – except for the one thing he really longed for – led to the demands for the most unreasonable and impossible requests, which only the good retainer and general factotum could satisfy, and if not, deflect or defer. Without a second's hesitation, Dim Son pressed for his guard, who took his order

and went to fetch Madame Shoo. Dim Son picked up the black book again, secreted it inside the Onesie and waited, his plastered pate lit by the low winter sun.

PAWN MOVES

Flur S. Ence was put on the spot – her Purification Overseer had taken her to one side and informed her that Madame Shoo had requested that she come to see her that same afternoon for a preliminary discussion on the forthcoming meeting with Chief Boddle Vascher. Not only that, but she was explicitly told by the PO not to inform anyone, repeat anyone. Flur S. Ence winced at the relish Klusch took in the emphasis given to anyone, signifying, as it did, who he had in mind.

She would have to do as bid, she knew that, but at what price? It was in less than two hours. What could she do? Should she tell Chief Boddle Vascher; after all he was her boss, her official supervisor and, strictly speaking she owed her professional loyalty to him and to him alone. A summons from Madame Shoo however, provided there was no sinister motive, was a high honour, almost too great and onerous for the young woman.

She doodled instead of getting script down and was unable to concentrate on what she should be doing. Finally she had her mind made up; she'd go up to Chief Boddle Vascher's office at short break as that was the single opportunity to get away without arousing Klusch's suspicious. As if reading her thoughts Klusch called across to her.

'May I suggest we go to the canteen together at break,' adding, 'I have some rather pressing questions on the second part of the mountain scene.'

Flur S. Ence had little choice and nodded her assent and abandoned all hope of getting to see the Chief. Maybe we can meet afterwards, she consoled herself, and her conscience.

DEADLINE

Madame Shoo's meeting with Dim Son, the first extended one since his return, was long and arduous. For the first half hour she had to endure his clowning around and endure his pretending that he didn't want to hear anything she had to report on, putting on a pout and, in uncooperative teenager mode, making constant interruptions. Madame Shoo had no choice but to persist in her reports on the affairs of State, ensuring that all matters of import in his absence were recounted: cultural and economic issues, security activity (that one usually got his attention), dealings with personal (not many of those) and professional lobbyists, as well as a host of budgetary and administration items, all of which had to be enumerated. If the world stopped tomorrow, Madame Shoo had resolved that any final judgement would show she had performed her duties to the letter right up to the end.

In the brief silence after the official business had been concluded, Madame Shoo presented the relevant documents for Dim Son's scrawl. In the middle of this Dim Son abruptly asked: 'What about the TV series? I haven't seen it on the box.'

'Oh that. You mean the *new* series Dim Son?'

'When's it on?'

The last thing to do was to attempt to contradict him, which left the alternative: distract and divert.

'Oh, I didn't think you wanted to see it until it was in full production. My apologies, I will contact the production crew today and see if we can arrange a pilot viewing.'

'We won't see if they can arrange anything; order them to be ready.'

'I'm sure they will get something ready. They had better have, as they can't say we haven't been generous with our resources,' she couldn't resist throwing in the wobbler.

'Resources? What resources?' Dim Son turned and looked at her.

'It's a well-known fact that Vascher eats up his annual resource budget before the end of Q2 each year.'

'Well, I will chew him myself if he doesn't produce the goods.'

'I'll see to it Dim Son.'

Madame Shoo knew that she had Dim Son off her back for

the time being and that was all she ever tried to do; there was no point whatsoever in revealing the real world to this fellow as it would only cause rampage, and she would be the first one trampled underfoot in his stampede of fury.

'If that's all I'll go and arrange it. What time suits best for the preview?'

Dim Son wasn't listening, his mind having become distracted by a pleasant memory from the recent hunting expedition; a scene by a wooded brook, where he had snared an XL, catching her by the hoof and lassoing her and then mounting while biting into the soft flesh of her shoulder, luxuriating in the taste of fresh blood and the aroma of mountain herbs reaching his nose.

A LIFELINE

Flur S. Ence's dilemma was out of her hands, or was it? The shared telephone on the table rang and Klusch rushed to answer it. Eyes, threatening, he looked over at her before slowly handing over the receiver, pressing her hand meaningfully as she took it from him.

'Yes?' Flur S. Ence listened to Chief Boddle Vascher's voice while Klusch glowered.

'Yes.'

Before she could speak the line clicked and Flur S. Ence was left with her mouth half open. Doing her best to retain her dignity and breathing as slowly as she could, she replaced the receiver.

'I've been called to Chief Boddle Vascher's office,' she said to no one in particular, avoiding Klusch's stare and aware that the people in the office had picked up on the tension and were listening. She calculated that Klusch could not interfere; even so, he stood up and, while not barring her way, was making a manful effort at looking intimidating, and put his index finger to his lips as she passed him by. She could feel the force of his stare and the inquisitive eyes of the others on her back as she moved through the crowded office on her way to the stairwell, but he didn't follow her.

As she made her way up the stairs, Flur S. Ence was certain that Chief Boddle Vascher hadn't been invited to this afternoon's meeting and it was unlikely that he even had wind of it; Klusch was probably already on the phone to Madame Shoo now, informing her that she was on her way to Chief Boddle Vascher.

What could she do? She daren't upset Madame Shoo but she had a strong sense of loyalty – and duty - to her boss. Nobody had warned her that work could like that and she would have far preferred to be getting stuck into the scripts but she also knew she couldn't change any of that now and had to somehow straddle the conflicts which raged beneath the surface of the Ritz.

PLOTTERS EVERYWHERE I LOOK

I've got a plan at last – das hat gedauert mein Freund – yes, I have a plan and it's not a bad one; with any luck this should keep me going until retirement, or the chute in the basement – whichever comes first. What a piece of luck having Flur S. Ence on board; she's a rock of sense, knows her stuff and it works out perfectly in the current scenario. She's going to get a bit of a surprise but I think I can pull it off.

I was beaming when she came in, thumb and index arranging my moustaches gently into shape. I had taken up the preferred position: chair set to maximum lean, legs on the desk, close to horizontal, a sure sign that I was in optimistic mood and *frech* to boot. At my rolling hand signal she took her place on the chair opposite – nervousness etched in her movements and expression.

'Is anything the matter?' I asked.

I'm not an emotional man, not anymore, but let me tell you, when I saw her enter my office, my *Gleichgueltigkeit* vanished and I sprung to attention and resumed the vertical. A damsel in distress, now there's something to marshal Chief Boddle Vascher's considerable resources. She was pale and there a tremor played on her lips – sweet, perfectly shaped, light purple lips. She appeared to be on the cusp of crying, as indeed she was.

'*Bitte, bitte,*' I consoled in a soft voice, full of genuine concern, 'relax my dear and I'll give you a beaker of Erika's *Apfelschorle*, that always works for me.'

She did my bidding and sat there, her tidy little body, all compressed into a trim figure. I thought it best to be quiet, even though, as you well know by now, that is a difficult *Aufgabe* for yours truly, but I did manage it.

She hardly had the strength to raise the glass to her mouth and I had to prompt her a few times and each time I did so she mechanically took a sip of the amber liquid. I wasn't to know at the time that the poor girl was in an horrific bind, unable to decide whom to tell what to, or whom not to tell what to. Don't ask me what decided it – it may have been the *Apfelschörle*, although I doubt it, delicious and all as it is. It may have been that I was the first to talk to her; I have no idea and I dread to think how it might have evolved if I hadn't made that fortuitous phone call.

At last she raised her head and gave me that look people give you when they know that you won't be delighted with what they are about to say. At the same time conviction was discernible; apparently she had made up her mind and was about to pour forth, come what may.

It was my turn to lose colour as she brought me up to speed and, old campaigner that I am, did my damnedest to disguise the unease – and growing fear – that clawed at my intestines. *Verdammte Hexe*; so that's how Madame Shoo wants to play it. Fine then, lay on and damned be him or her who first cries, 'Hold, enough'. I was out of my Grade 7 chair in no time and paced up and down my two meter track in military fashion. I was thinking hard, my spleen was active, 'fight or flight' mode had been activated; I was on the warpath.

'Interesting my dear,' I squeaked, knowing now that I had to somehow imbibe Flur S. Ence with a confidence that I myself scarcely believed in, otherwise it was curtains, or at the very least venetian blinds, for me. Typical, just when you thought everything was going swimmingly – which reminds me, just what was that Master Plan I called her up here to discuss? No idea... blank – the edifice starts to shake and the dust of crumbling certainties presage an impending disaster.

'I understand the position you find yourself in,' I said

without the slightest irony, 'but let me reassure you, I have been in very similar situations, oh yes, early on in my career.' Lo and behold, that last remark, seems from this distance to be the moment when Flur S. Ence transformed from a colleague to a trusted companion.

She was listening now and came out of the stupor she was displaying when she entered my office. I sensed a turning of the tide, ever so slight as it might have been, but the bleeding had stopped, so to say. She didn't speak, nor did I wish for her to say anything just yet, as it could only be a series of questions, the answers to which I almost certainly did not possess. Keep talking, I told myself, the patient is coming out of a state of shock, coax them back to *terra firma* slowly. And that is what I did, but I'm not going to bore you dear reader with the predictable, soothing palaver of corporate politics, personal envy, deviousness and betrayal... that is an endless list and after all, and it isn't a *verdammter Roman* I'm writing.

My ministrations did have their effect though, and soon I could see the scales of innocence dropping away and fresh insight dawning on my young friend. She was no fool, as I have said repeatedly, and the broad picture I painted for her had logic and credibility. Flur S. Ence was a fast learner and while I couldn't, at this stage, bank on a canny political ally at my side, I did entertain the hope of retaining my key intellectual resource.

In a funny sort of way Flur S. Ence, by being in my office and without doing anything, was almost obliged to stay in my corner, not that I'm implying that she had the intention of doing anything else – those thoughts are for another day. Now, before you even think it, I am not overly fixated by paranoia – I do have my moments (doesn't everyone?), but I generally take a realistic view; it's strictly business after all. Ha, ha, *ausgezeichnet*!

'What am I to do?' she, not unreasonably, enquired.

'Just leave everything to Chief Boddle Vascher,' was my equally reasonable reply, 'don't mention this conversation, and should you be asked about it, I suggest you reveal only those aspects that we are now going to embark upon.'

Both she and I knew that Madame Shoo would already have been informed by our friend Klusch that we were in session and we would have to live with that, so we set about tightening up some detail on one of the opening scenes of the pilot episode – a damn good one if I may say so. This made sense and when Flur S. Ence returned to her desk she'd be carrying a sheaf of loose pages from our brainstorming session, and the further beauty of it was that these modifications and revisions meant a hefty piece of transcribing and a plethora of administrative tasks for Klusch. Vascher, *bist du klug oder was?*

CAT & MOUSE

Flur S. Ence descended the staircase, lightened of the mental burden she had carried up with her, encumbered instead with the amount of paper and 'background material' that Chief Boddle Vascher had heaped into her arms as she left. 'These will distract him, mark my words,' was his parting shot as she backed out through the doorway. Klusch taking her aside today had been a watershed moment, and while she felt grateful for the psychological support that Chief Boddle Vascher's reinforced positive messages gave her, more importantly, an innate mental toughness began to assert itself.

Klusch's eyes clamped hold of her as soon as she entered the office. Taking the initiative – something new for her – she called out in tones of being put upon, 'we'll have to go through all of these for the Chief,' adding after a choreographed pause, 'lots and lots of changes and he wants them completed by the end of the week. Pressure from on high!' Chief Boddle Vascher, had he witnessed the brief exchange, would have been proud of her.

She was aware of Klusch's stare, even though she avoided eye contact and remained casual throughout a brief verbal exchange. He muttered something and after a few false starts silence returned. Flur S. Ence sat at her desk, going through the large sheets of multi-coloured brainstorming scribble on the table in front of her, perusing, selecting, discarding and sorting, doing just what she normally did, and it worked perfectly as a shield from any move Klusch might have been thinking of making.

'Did he ask you anything?' Klusch eventually hissed.

'How do you mean?'

'You know, what we spoke about?'

Flur S. Ence looked at him, the uncomprehending puzzle of a face exuding innocence and guilelessness. He couldn't be sure – in his mind all his peers had the potential to be enemies of one sort or another - but the look calmed his anxieties.

He had agonised on whether to call Madame Shoo, and eventually decided not to as she would have wanted to know why he hadn't done so immediately. Indeed he *had* thought of doing so but felt he might have been berated for not using some subterfuge to prevent the visit to Vascher. He was clearly uneasy and kept darting looks at Flur S. Ence, in the hope that he could in some way read into what had gone on upstairs.

His anxieties faded soon enough however as Flur S. Ence distributed the material she had brought with her from Vascher's office; there was a mountain of work to complete before Madame Shoo's progress meeting with the Chief. This didn't really bother Klusch one way or the other as his measurements were almost entirely contrary to that of a regular script writer; his bonus resting on the information he delved out and served up to his masters.

Flur S. Ence, despite her act, was anything but reassured, she still had the prospect of the meeting with Madame Shoo that very afternoon, a meeting without agenda or subject matter. Vascher had made clear to her that here be dragons, but had made her no wiser than that.

TYRANNOSAURUS SEX

Dim Son had resumed his workout sessions and pestered Madame Shoo about everything from Vascher's TV production to progress on the rocket front. That was another visit to be arranged, to see how the crazy rocket scientists were progressing in the basement their very existence was known only to the very few - a cabal whose members never left.

When he wasn't in conclave with Madame Shoo he was to be found in the library, advancing his education on everything from the desires of the flesh through to being and nothingness. His mind wandered from thoughts on the scientists down below to the transubstantiation of the body and in his mind there was a connection in the sense that he had convinced himself that advances in one area threw light on the other.

Dim Son perceived the Vascher project as a bridge between science and spirituality – his version of spirituality - which could be described simply as the attainment of immortality. Vascher's depiction of the birth of the dynasty, the interplay with natural forces and the mastering of those forces, was but an interim step in the phases of biological cybernetics that would lead to Dim Son's ultimate goal.

In the meantime, he thumbed through an old copy of Playboy, his attention caught by a set of leggy blond triplets, whose *derrieres* were cocked high and their cheeky come-on faces looked over their respective shoulders at the camera. It was uncanny, he thought, that the three sets of eyes looked just as if they were the eyes of a single person. More grist to the mill; more evidence that human characteristics could be transferred or manipulated beyond their physical limitations. A warm glow suffused Dim Son as he contemplated the glossy high-definition photos on the comfortable settee.

SUCCESSION PLANNING

Madame Shoo had an unexplained uneasiness, and found it difficult to pin down its origin. After all she was just meeting with the equivalent of an intern and there was no reason for the person holding all the trump cards to be edgy, she reasoned, but when she examined her motivation she had an insight: she wanted something; she had skin in the game. She wanted Flur S. Ence to work for her, and some intuition told her that this relative lowly employee could indeed be her successor. She recognised something of herself, something so far back to be almost forgotten; a young woman spotted by Daddy Kühl and snatched from oblivion to serve in the inner circle of power.

Madame Shoo had not softened over the years, but there was a smoothing out of the iron-willed personality. Perhaps it had to do with the transition to Dim Son's reign; however, there was more to it than that. Yes, she thought, all things must pass, myself included.

Flur S. Ence, whose background was impeccable – she had checked – was as close as she had ever come to identifying a successor and it would come down to how she managed the situation. Dim Son was a hurdle, but not the only one. As she sat alone in the gathering dusk, her final thoughts were on how to elicit from Flur S. Ence what was really going on within Vascher's project and the part she played in its development.

ON THE EVE

We're in the thick of it now, I can feel it. Mark my words, the whole caboodle is going to be put to flame, the edges will singe and burn and only those with fortitude and daring will survive, and there is only one way to do that – get down into the furnace. I will leave that little observation for later on in the telling of my story, but I want you to remember it and, if you should choose to judge me, you should know that events foretold did come to pass.

Madame Shoo's pawn shuffle had surpassed my calculations and surprised me; I grant you that. We aren't talking about any old pawn here; this one is going all the way and will be crowned at the other end; there's no doubt about that. And I will confess, it did up my regard for Madame Shoo; I could see a kindred spirit capable of spotting talent when it popped up and I knew that she also would make it to the top. New York, New

York.

But at this moment I was in a deadly game with the same Madame, a game I dare not lose. I might not win it, and, let's face it, I was unlikely to do so, but I did have the possibility of achieving a stalemate. I put away the hair dryer, with which I had fanned my face and fluffed out my moustaches and, if I may say so myself, they looked magnificent: imposing, imperial even.

Flur S. Ence should be proud to have someone of Generalissimo bearing fighting her corner. Wait a minute Vascher, 'fighting her corner?' Is that really what you are doing, or are you fighting your own corner with a promoted pawn? Hmmm. You see, I must ask myself these questions; it is only through this internal interrogation that I can reach into the heart of the matter.

INTO THE DEN

Flur S. Ence felt the pressure. She was on the horizontal escalators that would eventually bring her to the DMZ and then on to the meeting with Madame Shoo. Physically she remained calm but her thoughts, like gadding insects, annoyed her and jabbed at her. She tried everything: closing her eyes, clenching her fists, slowing her breathing, but, if these things helped at all, the difference was hardly perceptible. She was on her way to the eyrie and wished she weren't. This was not an episode to boast about to the family; this was dangerous and unpredictable, and she knew it.

She stood at the side of the moving apparatus, allowing others to pass by in a blur; and watched those coming the other way – behind the Perspex glass between them – loom up and startle her as their spectres sped into sight and vanished almost immediately. She only had her outsized bag with her which contained the carefully written notes on the completed scenarios. She pretended to herself that the meeting was purely functional even though her gut knew this was not the case.

She arrived, and stood like a miniature, before the great doors of the service lifts directly across from the escalator; these would take her to the top deck, from where she had the long walk through to the far side of the DMZ. She pressed in among the trellises of melons and grapes and the lift started its ascent with a groan of reluctance.

VALLEY OF DEATH

I am not a man for pacific thoughts and I never fully relax; I chug along and entertain myself with my latest anxiety. This is so, this I have found to be the case. Oh, I'm not the only one who frets and struts and am acutely aware that I will be heard no more. What of it? Well quite a lot actually; it's what drives me. There you have it – a neurosis-driven, fragile ego, batting hopelessly against the wheel of time, just like any old common or garden hamster.

She was up there. Was it any wonder that I was nervous? I'd just have to sit it out, no knowing how it would go, she could disappear into the labyrinth of power and never be seen again, or maybe the old bag would have her imposed on top of me – no, not in that sense - and have me transformed into a lapdog. Now where was I?

You see, here's the problem - I have no one else but myself

to discipline my actions; even Shoo can't do that, not really. She gives hints, utters vague threats, but ultimately she is in my hands. *Hold right there Vascher!* I've landed on it. That's it, she wants to get around me, usurp my role – and who could blame her? She sees right through me – Vascher The Bluffer she calls me behind my back. And here I was innocently thinking that she was simply using Flur S. Ence as a sounding post, a secondary source of information on progress, something to help her manage the narrative with Dim Son. How naïve I am. Nothing less than a move to take my Queen (to be) is what's on her mind.

Oh no Shoo, *no pasaran!* While Vascher retains his grey matter you cannot succeed, not over my (I hesitate to say) dead body. No, no, no. I'll grant the wrinkled old bag this much – she forces me to think. Okay Boddle, *immer mit der Ruhe,* get a grip on reality, assess the situation, create a risk profile and plan your next set of moves. You will need to be on your toes for this one.

And so to bed. Now, hold on a minute. Bed is postponed. There is work to do. How can I hold on to Flur S. Ence? That's what it boils down to. People get demoted and promoted all the time, we all know that and it probably underlays all that confounded office politics. Take me for example, riding high with Daddy Kühl and then he pops off; next thing you know I'm in the service lift moving my own cartons down the decks.

I wasn't resentful, I wasn't proud, I didn't get mad and I didn't get even – I planned to get ahead. You laugh? But I beg you, *bitte*, look at my situation: I was down on my luck, I may even have been a chute candidate, but what did I do? I rose like the Phoenix; I asserted myself in front of that dribbling lump of jelly and I received a positive reaction.

I did that, I'll have you know, not Madame Shoo, not Flur S. Ence. It was I! Deep breaths, keep a calm scabby head, bring it all back home. There you are Boddle, *wie ein frisch geborenes Kind,* ready for action. Now, I think I've talked myself into a better frame of mind; I'm my own analyst and motivation coach. I have it out with myself and voilà, I come on the other side of despair and ready for combat. *Kanonendonner ist mein Gruß!*

TEMPTING

A security screening operation, along with a paraphernalia of moving carousels, containers and metal detectors had to be negotiated when she came out of the lift. She was the only foot passenger; all the others were service personnel bringing foodstuffs and other supplies, and were shepherded through a separate entrance, a huge hall packed with security staff, a group of whom she saw going through a crate of melons one by one. She waited where she was after been processed, not knowing what to do until a brusque guard tapped her on the shoulder and pointed in the direction of an unsigned door. When she passed through she was met by a phalanx of soldiers - all twice her height. To make matters worse they clicked their submachine guns as her appearance triggered a state of alert. Nothing was said.

A disembodied voice called out, 'Here!' and she followed

or tried to follow the sound, having to make her way around the soldiers. A small cubicle came into view and she could see an impatient person inside a kiosk directing her with a rubber-gloved hand. She passed her papers through the gap at the bottom of the window, the official scrutinised it and handed the documents back to her. Again there was silence and Flur S. Ence found herself for the third time awaiting instructions.

'Through the door,' the man spat out, pointing behind her. Flur S. Ence almost stampeded through the door and came out at the other side to see the figure of Madame Shoo leaning against a pillar, her hands folded across her clipboard. She moved immediately in Flur S. Ence's direction and reached out and took her satchel.

'I decided to come and collect you personally,' she informed Flur S. Ence in a sweet, friendly voice, 'it can be a bit of a nightmare getting out of here. Everything go alright?', she asked, turning her head briefly in Flur S. Ence's direction without once pausing in her military step in the direction of her offices.

'Good, that's the worst of it behind you,' and then added conspiratorially, 'as long as Dim Son is in the best of moods.'

Flur S. Ence tensed; she hoped she wasn't meeting Dim Son, that was something she had not calculated for.

'But not to worry,' Madame Shoo continued as if sensing

Flur S. Ence's nervousness, 'he's in the library doing his research or whatever it is he does in there. Now tell me, how are *you* getting on since we last met? Making progress on the new production?'

Having said this, Madame Shoo allowed her eyes to rest on Flur S. Ence's face to see if she could read anything into the young woman's reaction. Vascher was a waste of time and only spun webs of obfuscation whenever she tried to delve into what he was up to. However, it wasn't by subterfuge or poker playing techniques, but by the pure simplicity of stating the facts that Flur S. Ence revealed no clues about happenings down in the studios.

'Yes, we are making good progress and the script is well advanced at this stage. A number of the early episodes are almost ready to start shooting.'

Script is one thing, Madame Shoo thought, but putting together a full production is another, however, she resisted the temptation to ask what was meant by ready to start.' Too early, might frighten the colt.

'You do most of the scripting, am I right?'

'Yes, that is correct,' Flur S. Ence answered, 'but of course Chief Boddle Vascher is the artistic architect and inspiration.'

'Oh, I see,' Madame Shoo replied, adding in a voice only heard by herself, 'that's another of his titles in the long list I suppose.'

'Everything on schedule?"

'I think so.'

'You think so?'

'Well, I don't look after the schedule. Chief Boddle Vascher does that I think.'

'That's the second time you've said, 'I think," Madame Shoo's stern mode surfaced and Flur S. Ence blushed.

'Don't worry about it,' Madame Shoo cut in quickly, I'm sure he's on top of his brief.' And as an afterthought, added, 'We'll find out soon enough.' The latter statement made Flur S. Ence look directly at Madame Shoo, something in the tenor of voice putting her on the alert.

They passed through a maze of carpeted corridors and Madame Shoo led the way into her office, dropping Flur S. Ence's satchel on her desk and she pressed a button on her intercom.

'Elevenses for two, thank you.'

She came forward again and with a regal extension of her hand pointed Flur S. Ence in the direction of some easy chairs and a low table by the large porthole window at the far end of the office which looked out on the upper end of the gorge, taking in the forests and mountains beyond. It was a magnificent view; the sweep of the unspoilt countryside visible from the window which took up almost an entire external wall of Madame Shoo's office. Flur S. Ence, even though she had been in the Ritz for a number of years, had never seen such an impressive sight.

'You like it?' Madame Shoo's question startled her; everything startled her; she had been on tender hooks ever since the invite.

'A little bit different from down below, don't you think?'

Flur S. Ence nodded weakly. She didn't quite know how enthusiastic a nod to give, afraid that to be too effusive was in some way betraying her colleagues. As for Madame Shoo, she was more animated than usual and, although unaware of it, briefly blushed in the presence of this relatively innocent young woman as motherly feelings came unbidden. Normally these were suppressed immediately but today she was in expansive form, concentrated as she was in defining the shape of the world around her.

Flur S. Ence had only answered the questions put to her and Madame Shoo could see that it was going to be difficult to get a conversation going. She sat down beside the girl and whispered in her ear: 'I felt just like you when I first came up here. You don't believe me but it's true. I was just a young woman like yourself when I was first installed –that's not the correct word I assure you – as a clerical assistant in the administration. That was in Daddy Kühl's reign of course,' here she paused and it looked to Flur S. Ence as a tone of regret and longing entered her speech, 'yes, different times now; different times requiring different people,' she concluded, her voice trailing off. After she had allowed this to sink she added in a whisper, 'and I won't be here forever.'

Flur S. Ence dismissed the last throwaway as absurd and her system blocked it out, but the 'absurdity' surfaced as fact a few seconds later.

'Do you think you would like to work here…working for Dim Son himself?'

There was no way Flur S. Ence could get past this one, no nod of the head or shy shuffle of the shoulders that sufficed; she had to answer the direct question.

'What about the…?'

'What about what?'

'The project.'

'Oh that. Vascher is an experienced producer, isn't he? He shouldn't have any problem replacing a screen writer. I don't mean to denigrate your work or what you can accomplish down below, but do you think it compares with what is on offer here?'

Flur S. Ence's discomfort up to this point was dwarfed in comparison to how she now felt. Madame Shoo wasn't beating around the bush; she was being offered a job on the top deck – it didn't get any higher in KRAK. Thoughts spun in her head as she looked for the safe harbour of a rational analysis of what was facing her. She couldn't stop a twitch in her shoulders and a deep blush had developed across her neck.

A knock came to the door; the Elevenses ordered earlier, Flur S. Ence thought, but no, it was a messenger in military garb. As soon as Madame Shoo saw who it was she sprung up and approached him. A short, whispered exchange of words followed and was concluded by a nod from Madame Shoo, a click of the heels and a rapid salute from the messenger.

'Sorry about this but I have to go and see Dim Son right away. I shouldn't be long, the refreshments I ordered will be here any minute. Please feel free to help yourself – there's no need to wait on my return. Right, see you shortly,' she concluded and was gone.

OH, OH!

I wonder what her approach will be; she's a clever old cow, moves cautiously, probably putting her toe in the water to see what temperature Flur S. Ence shows; hard to tell, verdammt hart, but I'm certain she is plotting to get Flur S. Ence under her wing. I wonder why? I'll probably never know. Maybe she's sick? Could be and she's foraging for the next Dalai Lama. That would be her alright, seeing herself as a line of continuity in the service of the State. Yes, she might be setting herself up for an orderly retirement, probably finds the whelp a bit of a chore. And could you blame her? What age is she now? Not the youngest, she seems to have been around forever - not that I can talk.

It's all very good speculating down here, but Flur S. Ence is up there right now having her ear filled with whatever promises and enticements Madame Shoo is offering. The girl is young and inexperienced and ripe for manipulation. You don't say! Oh I know she's clever, straight to the top sort of person; I saw that right away and if I'm honest with myself I can't but see Madame's machinations as any different from my own. Maybe that would be a better approach? Yes - what could I do, what could I offer?

Good question. First off, I like to look at motivation and then I like to get a feel for the timing. On the former, I have little enough information but let's say the scenario I mentioned above is being acted out. Fair enough, Flur S. Ence would be an asset in any part of the organisation and that includes the office of Dim Son. No doubt about it, in time she could take over the functions of tight ass herself.

The timing bothers me though. Why now? Shoo knows full well that the girl is up to her jam jars in a pet project personally authorised by the young pup himself (thanks of course to the divine intervention of my good self). Oh that was a moment, I could watch reruns again and again. I'll just have to wait for the debriefing but this waiting and not knowing is killing me. Must find a way to pass the time.

The script? Come to think of it I haven't reviewed it with Flur S. Ence for several weeks; I suppose it might be an idea to get back into some sort of *'schaffe, schaffe'* mode. I told her to come and see me immediately. Was that a good idea? Maybe not, Shoo has her spies everywhere. Hmm, I'll start off with a discussion on the script, that will help her relax... mustn't show panic or anxiety, that might only drive her into the arms of the skinny bitch.

Now, an entirely other thought arises – what if I were to encourage Flur S. Ence to take up whatever is on offer? That'd put the cat among the pigeons *and* I'd have someone on the inside track. Hoho! Or maybe not, she'd probably have forgotten about me before she went through the doors of the DMZ.

Now that's not fair; I see something in Flur S. Ence, a solidity, a groundedness, a good deal of uncommon sense for someone of her relative tender years. But the idea is worth playing around with. Only problem is we'll be left with the only scriptwriter worth her salt making tea for that fat slob.

Oh my gosh, no, *nein, um Gotteswillen nein,* that's just what's going to happen! Why didn't I see it before this; the bitch is doing it for that bastard? He'll have her in his harem before you could say cunnilingus. Oh, a fate worse than death. Time for the knight in shining armour to save the day; roll back those moustaches Boddle and summon your inner Sancho Panzo – we have a noble quest before us if we are to save the fair maiden.

JUST A NIBBLE

For several minutes after the unexpected summons for Madame Shoo, Flur S. Ence, alone in the large room, began to feel very uncomfortable now that the presence of her host wasn't there. Her head was in a tizzy and she tried, and failed, to make sense of what she was getting involved with. She couldn't put together a single coherent response on how to deal with the situation.

Her thoughts turned to her parents, that industrious little couple who toiled away in the grocery shop to this day, long after they should have retired to an easier pace of life. Flur S. Ence knew only too well the sacrifices they had made when she was selected for the higher education programme up at the Ritz and saw through the façade but never uttered a word to anyone, not even to her parents, although she suspected that they knew as well. Ever since there were only the special privilege days when she was allowed down to the city on a daytime-only leave just four times a year.

Her reflections were interrupted by a second knock at the door followed by the entrance of two waiters and a trolley displaying two cloched plates of food. They rolled the trolley across the carpet to a dining table on the other side of Madame Shoo's desk and one of them pulled back a chair and waited for Flur S. Ence to come across and take her seat. With an elaborate gesture, both raised the cloches simultaneously and left.

Flur S. Ence looked at the plates and didn't recognise any of the food displayed. Should she eat or should she wait? As if to answer her question, one of the waiters popped his head inside the door and said, 'Madame Shoo stated that it is perfectly in order for you to commence eating before her impending return.'

'Thank you,' Flur S. Ence croaked in response.

And she did, carefully lifting the tiny morsels with her chopsticks and experiencing unknown tastes, none of them unpleasant. Sour, sweet, spicy, piquant, vol-au-vents, inky mushrooms, tomatoes bleeding red juice and as sweet as honey. She completely forgot herself in the tumult of tastes had almost finished when the door opened and the waiter reappeared.

'Everything in order Madame?'

Flur S. Ence looked at him and looked around, wondering

if Madame Shoo had returned by some other entrance, but no, he was addressing her directly.

'Yes, thank you. Thank you very much.'

'Excellent Madame, the mistress has exquisite taste but, between us, she doesn't eat very much – however, it is more than made up for by Dim Son, ha-ha. Do you realise that you have just been eating the same food Dim Son had an hour ago?'

Flur S. Ence stared blankly at the waiter.

'Yes, but he has a rather more advanced appetite than yourself, no slight intended Your Ladyship,' he chuckled as he came to collect the empty dishes.

'Your drink will be brought in presently. Madame Shoo apologies for the delay; one can never tell how long an interview with Dim Son will go on. Ah well, *Dieu et mon Droit*, what?' and with that he whirled around and was gone.

After the strange waiter had left Flur S. Ence took a deep breath and experienced a sense of well-being and comfort, the food having had a pleasing effect. Before she had time to ponder too long on this he was back again, this time with a long glass of orange-coloured liquid, which he placed on the table and with a stiff bow exited silently.

Was he the same one, Flur S. Ence asked herself, comparing the stiff, silent formality to the previous over familiarity? She sipped at the drink, again an alien taste but luscious and smooth in its tart fruitiness and it glided down effortlessly. She remained at the table, not knowing what else to do and for a brief instant wondering if there were surveillance cameras on the walls. She considered collecting her satchel from Madame Shoo's desk but was too timid to do so.

TAKING THE INITIATIVE

I racked my brains on all the assorted what-ifs I could bring to mind, but they made off before I could pin them down, proliferated like splitting atoms, and I got nowhere. I had to get out of the office and decided that I would wander down to the general area. Walk around they say, and it is good advice. Before taking off I stretched myself and yawned louder than a braying ass as I made my stiff descent down the stairs.

Ach, mein alter Spion was in situ; doing nothing of course. He hadn't seen me coming and jerked up and stuffed a piece of paper under his writing pad when he saw me. *Et tu Brute*?

'Hard at it I see, Klusch,' I opened, my voice dripping with unoriginal sarcasm.

'Yes Chief,' he mumbled, straightened himself and re-arranged his jacket. I noted that the tone of contempt was absent.

Good. At least he knows not to underestimate me anymore.

'Is your colleague around?'

'Do you mean Flur S. Ence, Chief?'

'Yes, whatever her name is – the other scriptwriter.'

'She's in a meeting Chief.'

'A meeting? With whom?'

Klusch looked at me from under his eyebrows and the face revealed the lie about to be served up.

'I've no idea,' he said casually, his courage returning, 'she doesn't share her diary with me.'

'Is that so?' I persisted, keen to keep the *Arschloch* under pressure, although I wasn't quite sure to what purpose. He remained silent, a sullenness pulled his mouth down at the corners, the lips pouted into a sneer.

'WELL FIND OUT,' I shouted at the top of my voice, and I laugh when I recall his reaction; he fell off his seat, oh he did, oh he did, after which there was a brief but intense silence in the room and I could hear botched attempts by the others in the office to stifle their sniggers. He scrambled to his feet and high-tailed, stumbled and ran towards the door as if a fire had broken out in the office. I twirled my moustaches and looked around distractedly, exiting stage left with as much solemnity as I could muster.

THE PLANS OF MICE AND MEN

Dim Son was in the dumps and there wasn't anything, including gym and library sessions, to bring him out of it. The black dog was growling again and when that happened there was no rest for anyone; not until the dog had sated the pangs of loneliness and despair. He was indolent most of the time but when the big one hit he was prompted into action; only action could relieve the terrible and unbearable emptiness. Those around him had to dance to every tune; it started with the manservants who were tasked with impossible (and soon forgotten) requests and when that sequence was exhausted it was on to the one person at the Ritz who could help him bury the dog.

She had already seen him that morning and not noticed anything out of the ordinary, most likely because she was absorbed in her own plotting and Madame Shoo was a little surprised to be summonsed again so soon. As soon as she went in she saw immediately what the problem was, not that it could ever be discussed; Dim Son's bouts of depression were never addressed directly, only the working out of evasive action was on the agenda. Nothing for it, Madame Shoo thought to herself, but allow it run its course.

She stood still - a fixed, servile look on her face - in the middle of the room and even though she could see that he was aware of her presence, he made no move or gesture to initiate conversation even after she had declared herself at his service; he even turned his chair away from her in a sulk. She had to wait it out as she had learned from previous encounters.

Dim Son shuffled in his seat while Madame Shoo pondered on how to deal with Flur S. Ence waiting in her office; this current encounter could take hours. Madame Shoo was working to her own agenda and was concerned at the impression Flur S. Ence would have on being left on her own for an extended period.

Dim Son's issues had become secondary to her plans for the young woman, something that rarely if ever was the case and a development that would have consequences. Dim Son's hypersensitivity picked up any vibe like that in an instant, so Madame Shoo tried to think up of some excuse or other to get quickly back to her office and chided herself for not having sussed the situation that morning. She reasoned that she could handle whatever negative impact it had on Dim Son, as every little thing upset him when he was in this mood. Before she could act however, Dim Son spoke.

'Have you followed up with the television thing?'

'The project? Oh… everything's going smoothly; I have the script writer in my office right now,' she continued, seeing her chance of a diversion that fitted in with Dim Son's enquiry and her own need to get back.

Dim Son's baleful eyes looked up at her, 'I didn't know Vascher was coming up to your office on official business without my knowledge. Have you forgotten my edict so soon?'

'Oh no, not Vascher, Dim Son, he is the producer, or something like that; I'm talking about a young lady who accompanied him at our studio meeting some weeks back. Don't you remember?'

Dim Son grunted.

'Bring her here.'

It wasn't very often that Madame Shoo was nonplussed, but she was now. Why had she mentioned the young woman to him; she was losing her touch. This was very last thing she wanted and there was no way to directly refuse the request. She shot out impulsively.

'Oh, but I think she's probably gone back to the other side by now. I dismissed her so I could deal exclusively with your request for a meeting.'

'Less of that smarmy nonsense, bring her to me right now!'

'Yes, Dim Son.'

Madame Shoo bowed and took a breather as soon as she had pulled the door shut, prompting the sentry to look at her strangely, a look that she didn't like.

'What to do, what to do,' Madame Shoo called out to the empty corridor as she strode back to her offices.

SATISFACTION

Alright, alright, a bit over the top. Never show them your anger and all that claptrap. Breaking the rules is an essential component in anyone's survival kit bag, otherwise you're a slave, if not to others then to yourself. It won't be long until our friend Klusch is reporting back to headquarters, but it won't do him any good I'll wager. I have upset their source of information, but could they do anything about it? That's the thing about spies you see, as soon as they're rumbled they shrivel like squidging balloons; they go loopy with fear and spin off in any old direction at all. There they lie, exhausted and in crisis, wondering how it all happened, little realising that they have been led in a not-so-merry dance.

My big eared friend, you shall now duck, bob and weave to no purpose; you will become victim to staccato twitches until, like a spent cartridge - your bolt shot - you will twirl harmlessly into outer space. Please indulge me, yes, I know I'm gloating, but can you blame me? I do so laugh when I recall old Klusch slipping off his chair, his eyes almost popping out in panic and disbelief.

Oh yes, let me tell you, I simply must. I returned to my old hovel and gaily kicked papers and paraphernalia across the floor, cursing the lack of generosity in that confounded abode. It's true somethings sting deeper and, despite my light-hearted enjoyment at Klusch's expense, I still have plenty of time to nurture a deep seated resentment at my fall in status.

Whatever... let me rewind... yes, too much of a good thing. I laughed, oh how I laughed. It had been coming; his (Klusch I mean) sneering, his one over you attitude, all that had grated from the start. Scriptwriter my boondoon; I'm not even sure if he is literate. I suppose refinement of one faculty (in his case, the ears) may have a deleterious effect on the other functions.

Did I tell you what my parting words to him were? No? Well I shall repair the error forthwith.

'Do not return until you have located her and sent her to my office. DO YOU HEAR?'

He heard alright, even if he didn't answer. He only had time for the door knob as he fumbled it open, and all we could hear was his pounding steps as he retreated pronto down the corridor in the direction of the DMZ. Was I surprised? You're having a laugh surely? RETURN TO HEADQUARTERS was probably the bleating message tapping out in his cranial network. Get back to Mama. She may have thought she could capture my advancing pawn, but Her Majesty was about to experience a bit of blowback courtesy of yours truly. That's enough of that for now, better to curl the moustaches and wait around and see how the whole kaboodle comes crashing down.

A MESSAGE

Madame Shoo worked the next moves, laboured to anticipate the options that influenced later ones, the decisions that led down specific pathways; all was in play and the wished for uneventful stalemate was unlikely - no, impossible as it stood after her last encounter with Dim Son. This she knew from bitter experience and steeled herself against mortal thoughts. The colour on her face, never rosy, was a chalky white and she walked faster than she liked – not Madame Shoo's style at all.

She stopped and steadied herself against one of the corridor walls, but there was no need to be self-conscious; these corridors of power could be better described as vacuums of inertia and emptiness. She had to present Flur S. Ence to Dim Son – this was unavoidable – and it wasn't going to be enough, as in this mood he'd continue to find fault and reject every proposal.

She was well used to that, but the likely Flur S. Ence outcome bothered her more. A carefully planned and scarcely executed gambit was in danger of being blown out of the water, not from Vascher or any external agency but by the edifice whom she served. Time for cool heads she thought as she steadied herself and went to pass the bodyguard by her office door.

Just as she did so the sound of thundering steps came from the direction of the DMZ. Somewhat distracted as she was, she waited out of curiosity. It was a runner, coming in her direction, and her surprise and disbelief were complete when she saw the ungainly figure of Klusch, panting, spluttering and waving frantically, something of the drowning person about him. From his appearance, it appeared he must have run all the way from the other side and when he reached her he fell flat on the ground, sucking in great gulps of air and a display of painful grimace on his upturned face.

Madame Shoo assumed a melodramatic pose and pressed herself against the door that she had unconsciously closed again; an unbidden morbid fear of weakness rose up in her breast, her hands crossed her chest, clutched the clipboard and she stood frozen with her mouth open. Perhaps it was just as well that Klusch was consumed by his own exhaustion to notice, as had he done so, his belief in the omnipotent power of his de facto superior might have been damaged beyond repair.

Madame Shoo was the first to recover, brushing down her clothes with slow deliberate movements of her hands and clipboard and sweeping back a strand of hair and, with a voice of utter calm, asked: 'What brings you here Klusch? I don't think there is any need to emphasise how dangerous this is and, as you must know, it strictly contravenes the regulations under which you operate.'

Klusch looked up; the sound of the words and their content placed fear above exhaustion and in the blink of an eye he was on his feet with head bowed.

'A serious situation Madame,' he whispered and raised his head slightly, so that he was almost looking directly at Madame Shoo, 'he wants her back in his office.'

'He wants her back! Who wants who back?'

'Chief Boddle Vascher wants Flur S. Ence in his office now.'

It took a few seconds for Madame Shoo to take in what Klusch was saying, but then its impact seeped through to her evaluation of the situation and she whispered something to her bodyguard.

'Come with me,' she beckoned to Klusch and instead of following the bodyguard, she headed in the opposite direction and, standing before an unmarked door, took a key from her pocket and waved Klusch inside.

They were in some sort of library or document storage

area. The room had wall-to-wall shelving filled with boxes of grey binders, all labelled in thick red ink. Klusch didn't get much time to take in his surroundings as Madame Shoo was in his face.

'Now, tell me *everything*!'

Klusch did as bid, even describing Vascher's burst of temper – although he did omit the incident of falling over – and the order that Flur S. Ence be brought to his office immediately. Madame Shoo nodded as she tried to marry two conflicting demands: Klusch could not send Flur S. Ence to Vascher at the same time as she presented her to Dim Son. Something had to give; she made a telephone call.

SAFE HARBOUR

And show up she did. Less than a half hour after Klusch broke loose I heard a timid knock on my door and on my 'Herein' there she was. Brow beaten, I observed, and a face that normally didn't reveal much, looked as if it had been deafened and disoriented by barrages of close quarters rocket fire.

'Ah, there you are,' I greeted her as if it were a regular catch-up meeting, 'please, please, *bitte*, take a chair and rest yourself.'

Taking the lead was the best course of action and considering her shell-shocked look, I sallied forth, philosophising in the grand manner and throwing in the odd plot twist for our soap opera, but I could see that she wasn't listening, nor could I have expected her to do so. I realised that what I was attempting was akin to keeping a person from going into shock after an accident.

I had an image of myself – not unpleasant I must admit – kneeling on the ground and trying to revive her as she lay below me. My soothing words kept her *compos mentis,* and I knew with a little time she'd come back to me. And she did, and even more surprisingly, she pulled me up on one of my plot twists (after the abortive mutiny on board Daddy Kühl's ship), pointing out the contradiction in my logic.

'Quite right,' I agreed, '*ganz richtig*, that I hadn't noticed,' and then for fun I threw in an, 'I don't know what I'd do without you.' She ignored it. I'd have been disappointed if she hadn't you know; Flur S. Ence pops in at the top of the stack in my hierarchy of esteem. And then it was straight back to business.

'So, what does Madame Shoo want?'

'I think she wants me as some type of deputy manager in Dim Son's office.'

Well, I thought, no sugar coating the message there. Fair play to you Flur S. Ence, you move up another notch in my estimation. I suppressed a 'cheeky bitch' comment and then asked, as calmly as I could:

'And…what do *you* think about that?''

'I want to write scripts.'

Up yet another notch. That's my girl.

'For your own sake, is it?' Now I know, please, I know,

what kind of a question is that to ask the young woman, but I had to ask it.

She looked directly at me for the first time since coming in. Until then she had been focused on some undefined spot in mid-air, but now she *looked* at me. A bit disconcerting I must say, quite extraordinary. Terrific surge of electricity when those eyes met mine.

'I don't know if I can answer that question,' she answered, a serious tone of disclosure in her voice, so unmistakably clear that it answered the question all by itself.

'Not to worry,' I blurted, trying to hold down my own emotions, 'I understand.'

And I did, I really think I did. My bird had flown back home. As it must be clear to you, I had no idea at that moment what had preceded Flur S. Ence's arrival at my door. In my petty way I was just pleased by the perceived minor victory over Madame Clipboard, but as you may know from my dealings with that source, it would never be as simple as all that.

'Can I help?' I asked, in honesty not knowing why, as helping would not be my forte. Without a blink, Flur S. Ence shot back, 'Some support would be appreciated.'

Well now, what did I tell you, this young woman has something about her, speaking to her boss like that. I was doubly impressed: first I knew what she meant by 'support' and secondly, she stunned me with her candour. I had been inattentive, had been absent so to speak, had taken my eye off the ball so to say. To put it bluntly I had been acting the maggot, had become obsessed with my own difficulties, forever picking at old wounds and luxuriating in my perceived humiliations.

The girl had hit the bullseye and I had no option but to respond in like manner. Game playing was over and it was well past time that I made a stand for something. Getting out of the old habits was hard though and I had to suppress the urge to tell a tasteless joke, knowing that it might have hurt the girl more than I could ever understand.

'*In Ordnung... Du hast Recht.*' I mumbled, 'please tell me what type of support we are talking about. I know I have been remiss and I see clearly that it has been most unfair to you.'

She looked at me again, a look that clarified the meeting of minds, and confirmed that the shadow boxing was at an end, that preliminaries were now dispensed with. It took some time before she spoke and the silence in the room took on a spectral presence. I got slightly frightened if I may be frank. What *was* she going to say?

'This is a serious business I think,' she said, 'am I correct?'

'Depends on what aspect of the enterprise you are referencing,' I replied, fear in my gut.

'When I was in Madame Shoo's offices I got a different perspective and I'm not just talking about the carpets and furnishings up there.'

I looked around my dismal den, taking in the heaps of papers and books, the peeling lino, the dusty walls festooned with spider webs in the upper corners.

DIVERSION

Madame Shoo gave Klusch the third degree, made him feel uncomfortable in what had been a very uncomfortable morning; he could still feel the pain in his tailbone. She was looking at him but in her mind something else churned over and she didn't remove her gaze until she had resolved the dilemma.

'Come with me,' she ordered, sweeping past him and out the door.

They returned to her offices. Klusch began to fret - this did not look like a victory for his side; Vascher was getting what Vascher wanted. He opened his mouth but thought better of it and tried to make himself melt into the wall behind him. Madame Shoo, with determined stride, went to her desk and took up the telephone handset and made another call.

'Who is Chou Late's replacement?' She waited.

'Put me through to him.'

After Madame Shoo was connected she spoke in something akin to a coded language and Klusch had no idea what the discussion was about.

'How much time to do you need?' Pause.

'That's acceptable and make sure it's impressive, You know your audience.'

She sighed as she put down the receiver, momentarily forgetting that Klusch was there.

'You can go, I don't need you anymore.'

Klusch scooted out the door as quick as his legs could carry him and made his way to the DMZ, leaving Madame Shoo to prepare her story for Dim Son.

*

'Something has come up,' she said, remaining close to the door after her entrance.

Dim Son looked up; having forgotten why she was there.

'The rocket team have made a breakthrough,' and as Madame Shoo uttered her words, she wondered if it was wise to unholster such a big gun to deal with the absence of a lowly employee, sensing that Dim Son might have already forgotten his previous request. But the cat was out of the bag now. I'm losing my sharpness, she thought, and noted that it hadn't been the only lapse in recent times. She consoled herself with the thought that he might well have remembered his original request had she not made this diversionary move.

A half hour, the general had said. Plenty of time.

VASCHER REFLECTS

Anitwit? Too right. Although that is to assume that there is wit there in the first place, and I wouldn't take that as a given. Small brained, stupid, naïve, what have you, this guy takes it a step further – every time. Not just idiotic but an idiocy that invariably results in certain catastrophe, major or minor. To those of you who are sceptical or disbelieving of my account of happenings at the court of Dim Son, I beg you to please bear in mind that to those of us present there at that time, everything was stinknormal. Don't ask me how or why, and please look at this report as a personal, although by no means inaccurate account of the daily goings-on in his kinky kingdom.

I had become embroiled in the lunacy of it all and it had taken the courage and frankness of that slip of a girl to jolt me out of the long-running nightmare. Even in Daddy Kühl's time

KRAK had been far from a business as usual sort of place, but there had been a logic of some kind that underpinned the carry-on. Now we had reached the point where reality was obscured and it was not so much seeing through a glass darkly, as being encrusted in the amber of delusion. I am not just referring to the fat yob's madness, but the complete breakdown of human solidarity in the face of an unspoken – and mostly unseen – terror.

Surely I was a prime candidate for *Vernichtung? Jein.* There was a reason why I hadn't been exterminated: first of all, I had – you may be surprised to hear – quite a reputation for churning out top-class propaganda, *stets nach dem letzten Motto;* secondly, the legacy of my connection with Daddy Kühl should not be underestimated, even if it didn't save Chou Late and the others (but there were reasons for that). I have a suspicion that Daddy Kühl gave Dim Son some final orders; of course I have no way of knowing what they were and it's a waste of time speculating. My demotion, as it turned out, was a bit of a Godsend. Expectations were low and so far hadn't been exceeded. *Alles in allem, ich habe Glück gehabt.*

But in truth I was in a quandary; just looking at the expression of Flur S. Ence's face brought about a profound change in me, a change from which I could not retreat. I had entered a new stage of consciousness, if that is not a too highfalutin a phrase for what was beginning to manifest within me; no longer could I play the role of the perpetual rebel, forever kicking against the pricks.

This was *serious*; heads would roll – I knew that and, while you are at liberty to disbelieve me, my own head was not number one on the list of those I wished to save. Flur S. Ence had left my office despondent and defeated. She made as if to say something to me but then changed her mind and departed wordlessly, not even closing the door behind her.

My navel gazing completed, I rose, groaned and stretched myself. I gave a sharp twirl on my moustaches and went and closed the door, vehemently kicking some manuscripts to the side after they had almost tripped me up. *To wit to woo a merry note.* Anger was on the rise and I had to harness it. The guessing game was at an end – Madame Shoo had attempted to snatch my best employee, whether for her own benefit or because of some animus she held towards me. To be honest I couldn't tell and I was inclined to think that it didn't matter. The more serious question was – what did *I* want? And you may add to that – was I willing to commit to what I wanted?

The latter, if you knew me well, was by far the more difficult one to answer and I wasn't able to do so that afternoon. I spent the rest of the day in my cubby hole striding up and down all three steps along the boulevard of stacked books and periodicals, a-twirling and a-mooching, as distant as ever from grasping what I needed to do. As it turned out, and you shall see for yourself presently, events (my dear boy!) became the organiser of my thoughts and (eventually!) my tentative actions. I must rack my brain now and recount them to you truthfully when we next speak.

POISED

Madame Shoo didn't do panic, it just didn't fit with her nature to be excited or nervous and it very probably was the major reason she had held on to the position she occupied in KRAK. There was a sense of concentrated focus, like a magnifying glass seizing the sun's rays and using its power to burn through to what lay beneath. She assembled and processed thoughts, calculated standard deviations, computed the Pareto probabilities. Madame Shoo had never been caught out, never been compromised; the chances of her being without an exit strategy in any given situation were close to zero.

This was the case with her diversionary move on the missile demonstration – Dim Son had taken the bait, the shuddering power of rockets zooming off (to God knows where) was just the thing to jolt him out of his depression and with Madame

Shoo setting the pace, he wasn't going to come back to the Flur S. Ence subject for some time. And the interval could be used by Madame Shoo to continue to spin her next thread.

'I'll get the dressers,' she said and left before he could change his mind again.

Within minutes she had returned, with her battalion of ladies who immediately set about polishing, powdering and trussing Dim Son into the uniform of the Commander of land and sea forces.

'*Après, après,*' they tittered as he groped and fondled them during the changing procedure. Dim Son luxuriated being surrounded by a horde of women, the more the merrier, and reminisced on the pleasant memories of his recent soiree in the helicopter. On this occasion however his urges were kept in check - the women had their orders and they feared Madame Shoo more than they feared him.

'Is Chou Late meeting us?' Dim Son asked, taking Madame Shoo by surprise and she whispered in his ear the news that Chou Late had already received his Exit Document some months back.

'Oh, they're all the same,' he sighed, 'how am I supposed to keep an inventory of who's who in this damned set up. There's too many of them hanging on my coattails as it is. Remind me to issue a new batch of Documents when we get back from the military demonstration,' he concluded, having worked himself up to a bit of rightful indignation.

'General Stab is the man now,' Madame Shoo informed him as they made their way to the theatre, 'the same one who organised your last hunting expedition.'

'Him? Yes, a very good fellow, laid on a splendid array of vittles and flesh. Why didn't you tell me and I would have brought him a little present?'

'I have arranged, with your approval – that the entire missile section be granted an appropriate bonus and an official accolade for this significant milestone.'

'Quite right, splendid. These guys will get us the headlines we deserve.'

As they descended in the lift an old thought bubbled up in Dim Son's head, something to do with Vascher but just then the elevator doors opened and a loud shout was heard as the colour party stood to greet them. After the fanfare was through with there was a final blast of trumpets and an older man in full regalia – General Stab – approached and bowed. He had a twinkle in his eyes and was obviously on the best of terms with Dim Son.

'An honour, most gracious leader. An auspicious day in the unfolding of the continued rise of Mighty KRAK as we will presently see for ourselves.'

Dim Son silently acknowledged the elaborate greeting

and stood there waiting for whatever was to come next.

BROUGHT TO HEEL

Well, *mein alter Kumpel*, believe it or not, I cried real tears after she left. Don't ask me why, I certainly can't explain it, but a veritable torrent streamed down my cheeks, cascaded along the crevices of my wrinkled visage and converged in the thicket of my moustache before spattering on to the lino. It kept up for some time and when it concluded with the gradual diminution of heaving sobs, I was left totally and utterly exhausted. As I recovered my thoughts turned to the *Ursprung* of this cataclysmic outpouring. What could have caused it? No sooner had the thought hit me than another one sprung out like a cat and advised me to cease my search for the source of my sorrow; a wise thought, if I may say so.

It took some time, but recover I did and like the altered atmosphere after a heavy thunderstorm, the clouds dissipated and the view went on forever. Distant mountains – in my case, serenity of mind, came into sight and all that mental chatter vanished, allowing a pacific calm to enter deep into my very soul.

Without doing a damned thing I was perfectly happy to sit in my cell; Madame Shoo and Dim Son little more than grasshoppers on the edge of my inner vision. It wasn't a feeling of omnipotence, not at all; moreover a tiny smidgen of humility (I jest not!) made one of its rare visits to the conscious abode where it was welcomed like a new born babe. Vascher lost all his resentments, all his envy, all his bitterness – at least for those precious moments after the downpour. It didn't last of course and there was nothing in my power that could make it do so. *Och ja, das war herrlich mein Freund.*

Seated at my purloined Grade 7 chair, smiling like an idiot I was, when who should come by but my old adversary, Klusch. Who, you may well ask, was better suited at dumping one out of the most pleasant of daydreams? Never in my lifetime had I seen him anywhere near the vicinity of my cubbyhole. He was out of breath and looked as if he had been on the hoof since I last saw him struggling with the doorknob downstairs. A greater contrast you'd find it difficult to imagine; Vascher The Placid, grinning inanely in his oversized chair and a panting Klusch holding on to the jamb of the door, his eyes popping, his tongue lolling, and a strange, beseeching look on the asymmetrical angular face.

'Did she return?' he gasped, with a look that implored and feared all at once. I'm sure that if I had said that I hadn't seen her, he'd have collapsed on the spot, but I'm not a sadist (not really) and I had no wish to prolong the poor man's agony. I still basked in the fading ecstasy of my recent vision, needing to do little more than scratch my navel while watching the world go by.

'Indeed she did, Sir. I am indebted to your assistance in this matter and you may consider yourself free of all liabilities to my good person from this point onwards. Go therefore and guard the sparkling diamond we have in our midst and be assured of my eternal *Dankbarkeit*.'

To say that he gave me a funny look could not do justice to the contortions his face went through. It was as if I could see all of Euclid's theorems being projected there, a hologram of intersecting bone structures rearranged themselves in a frenzy of Rubik combinations; as if some internal physical force were analysing the calculations, interpretations and responses to what I had just said. At last the light show came to an end and Klusch, taking in that he had been excused, bowed silently and left.

SMOKES & MIRRORS

Dim Son's apathetic demeanour did not alter right through the 'demo'. He was looking at a computer simulation of a rocket being fired in pixelated slow motion over a landscape of regenerating vanishing points as they went towards an ever-moving but never-changing horizon. Eventually it dipped down at the upper left of the monitor and a series of white, cigarette-shaped shafts of white light consumed the entire screen.

General Stab cut in before the whole thing fizzled out, having watched his master's expression throughout.

'Just a simulation Your Excellency, but keep it in mind that your next demo will be out the chimney before you can say 'ready or not, here I come',' and with this he summoned up as hearty a laugh as he could. Dim Son looked confused but nodded.

Madame Shoo, who had been standing in the shadows, saw everything and made a note to thank the general for saving the day. This, after all, had been her idea and while it wasn't the real thing, it appeared to have worked as a diversionary manoeuvre. She could handle the fallout with Dim Son when they were alone, but at a minimum she had avoided a meeting she wasn't prepared for, and any possible secondment of Flur S. Ence.

As was usual in general company, Dim Son kept quiet and it was left to the general to smoothly conclude the 'demo' with a wave of his hand indicating a table laden with food and drink. Madame Shoo directed the rest of the crew and the waiters to vacate the room and served both men, knowing that this intimate gathering would further help restore Dim Son's equilibrium. The general kept up the patter, regularly laughing at his own jokes and while neither comfortable nor relaxed, Dim Son became amused enough to engage in conversation.

'A few months you say?'

'Yes, I should think so Dim Son, there is so much technology involved these days that it is but a few steps to move from concept – what you have seen today – to a viable transfer to real world hardware.'

'Concept?'

General Stab stuttered before answering. 'Not quite the

correct word Your Excellency... *prototype*, yes that's the word I was looking for.' he sighed in relief at having found a more suitable description, 'the simulation you've seen is an identical duplicate of the program which will launch the real thing.'

'Hmmm,' Dim Son looked unconvinced, 'then why couldn't we have the *real thing* today? That was what I was led to believe,' and as he said this he threw a calculated glance at Madame Shoo, who started to tap on her clipboard.

'Ah, a very good question Your Excellency and a splendid observation if I may add. Let me roll things back and explain the differential: what you have witnessed just now is a genuine simulation of the launch and deployment, an absolutely identical version to that embedded in the rocket itself. Now, we must remember that we are in the realm of mega tonnes of high explosives and to put that to the test we need to move carefully, very carefully indeed, and that is not even to take account of the cost. We have to be absolutely sure Your Excellency, *absolutely sure,* that we do not waste valuable material before taking that final step.'

Here he paused and held his finger up for emphasis, 'the greatest day in the history of *Mighty* KRAK is not far off,' and here he winked at Dim Son, 'I stake my career on it Your Excellency.'

'Very well, I look forward to that,' Dim Son replied, returning his attention to the delicacies, which Madame Shoo proffered at that moment.

'Could I fly in it?' Dim Son mumbled through his food.

Madame Shoo and General Stab looked at each other and she gave the general a signal indicating that he had better answer this one, before again sliding into the background.

'In what sense?' The general asked casually.

'Well, the running dogs have sent this sort of thing to the moon, have they not?'

'Oh I get you now Dim Son. ... yes, in the large scheme of things we could make a modification to enable human travel– indeed that capability is already built into the actual rocket itself, but for the present we like to concentrate on the explosive payload,' and with this he winked and nudged Dim Son, 'they don't like it up 'em, now do they Your Excellency.'

Dim Son looked more than a little puzzled but decided to laugh anyway – the general had that effect on him – then nodded at Madame Shoo to indicate that he wished to go, but before he departed he moved closer to General Stab and whispered something in his ear.

'Yes Your Excellency,' said the general and he bowed deeply to hide the grimace on his face.

Back in his quarters Dim Son knew he was forgetting something but he just could not recall what it was, his memory being no doubt impaired by Madame Shoo's intentional fussiness and business-like insistence on the procuring of edicts, signatures and the general everyday business. To cap it off, she suggested that he should take a nap after the activities of the day. A siesta came a close second to food in his hierarchy of needs and the opportunity for a little sleep rarely if ever failed to elicit his assent.

'Arrange an extra gym session when I wake up,' he called back to her as he went towards his bedroom.

'Yes Dim Son,' Madame Shoo chirped.

FOREBODING

So there I was, the prime instigator of the entire carambolage. What could I do? The time for tactical sniping, ducking and diving, was past. I had to pull something more substantial out of the sizzling embers. It's a truism I know, but necessity really is the mother of invention, and now was as good a time as any for yours truly to embark on what was going to be a frantic game of cat and mouse.

I took time to re-consider everything while still in the throes of that calm clarity that had taken root after the spontaneous cleansing of my countenance. Where was I positioned on the board? What obstacles did I have to overcome? Who my enemies were was clear enough: *Primus inter pares* being Madame Shoo and propped up behind her, Lard Arse, The Great Invincible Father, munching and riding his way to some infinite nirvana.

That evil bitch was on a quest. With her planned deployment of Flur S. Ence to the offices – I should really say harem – of Dim Son. an old initiation was being set in motion. There she was to be coached and readied by Skinny Mama herself and at the perfect moment, presented on a plate to the overweight and oversexed clown.

I'll bet a pound to a penny that my analysis is not far off; I do have precedent to guide me. What, you ask, was Madame Shoo's apprenticeship like? I'll let you guess. History, if you can call it that, was about to repeat itself. Unless, that is, I was prepared to be an instrument of diversion. A tremor went right through me; I knew well enough what that entailed. The more I thought about it, the clearer it was to me that I had a very limited number of choices, even if I were to take it as a given that I was a bloody fool to start with - a fool about to risk his life.

The Ritz Corral was a fortress for those on both sides of the structure, as I knew from my recent trip to Slag City, but now that Madame Shoo had got wind of that, my All Areas pass had been revoked and getting down to the Big Smoke again would be nigh impossible, and even if I got there, what then? Sepp Seife could be of some assistance, but a razzia of massive dimensions would be sent out to swamp the place. I could lie low for a while, I might evade the combing crew initially, but it was inevitable that the greater force would eventually succeed and within weeks at most I would be squeezed out like a toothpaste tube. And before I even go there, what of Flur S. Ence herself, did she want to go through all of that? You know I had never asked her; I didn't know her well enough to even broach the subject, but the time was approaching when we simply had to have a *Besprechung unter vier Augen*.

RUMBLED

Dim Son had an extended workout in the gym after his siesta; it ran on so long that Madame Shoo had to usher in a replacement troupe as the session went into extra time. Washed, showered and cosseted in his satin robe, he sat on the flipped-up recliner in the stateroom, his gaze catching his own reflection in the plate glass windows. He was pleasantly tired but refreshed after his siesta and workout. Then it struck him.

'The conniving cow, she spent the whole afternoon trying to divert me,' he said to the empty room. He almost rose up in anger but the force of gravity won out and he lay back and stretched out in the armchair. 'Well, two can play at that game,' he mumbled to himself, 'we'll see who's in charge here in the morning.'

With that he reached into an outside pocket of the dressing gown and brought out the little black book which he had retrieved from his bedside drawer. Flicking through the pages, he placed his thumb over a random piece of text.

If a man abides not in me, he is cast forth as a branch and is withered;

And men gather them, and cast them into the fire, and they are burned.

And then he began to sing gaily:

'U better watch out, U better not lie,

U better watch out, I'm telling U why

Madame Shoo, is goin' to go die,

Madame Shoo, is goin' to go die.'

He replaced the book and started to twiddle his thumbs slowly, every so often extending his right hand, thumb wavering, before making an exaggerated 'thumbs down' signal to the darkened windows. He kept repeating the gesture, guffawing and splurging with laughter as he did so.

THINGS MOVE QUICKLY

The two events happened simultaneously, a well-co-ordinated military operation under the direction of General Stab. Madame Shoo was arrested in the early hours and vanished from view. At exactly the same time Flur S. Ence was brought under guard to Dim Son's quarters. This time there was no pass control or security as she had already been strip-searched and issued with new clothing. After arrest, her cubicle was sealed and a guard stood on duty outside the door. At first it wasn't known what had become of Madame Shoo. Had she been executed? Was she in prison? No one knew and, as it transpired, later events overshadowed the matter of her fate.

'An accident has befallen my servant, Madame Shoo,' Dim Son announced to Flur S. Ence after she had been shown into his offices. He sat at his desk, figure averted and not looking Flur S.

Ence in the face. Flur S. Ence, still in a state of shock, briefly recounted her premonition when she had been in Madame Shoo's offices and she now understood the discomfort and fear she had first felt in this grandiose world.

'Very unfortunate without a doubt, but the world moves on, what?' he continued not waiting for comment. 'I need an assistant of the highest quality and I am happy to announce that – based on my own research, and Madame Shoo's recommendation, that you have been selected to join my household in her previous role. You have the final say of course, and if you do not wish to take up the offer you will be free to return to your assignments in the Cultural Ministry.'

Flur S. Ence took a deep breath and bowed in the direction of the portly figure sitting before her. Despite her inexperience, she knew that refusing Dim Son's offer was, to say the least, ill advised.

'I am honoured and humbled by your offer Your Excellency and only fear that I do not possess the necessary experience and faculties required for the onerous duties of this position.'

'Very good. We'll take that as a *yes* then. Unfortunately, Madame Shoo is not available to train you in, but I'm sure you'll soon find your way around and I will be on hand to offer my advice and guidance should you need it.' He paused and added as he got up, 'well that's all settled then. First thing I need from you is to have the gym prepared for my workout.'

And with that he left her standing, waving his hand at the door which slid open as he disappeared into his bedroom, leaving Flur S. Ence to wonder where the gym was and what preparations were necessary. Before she had too long to think about it, a guard, who had remained in the room, clicked his heels and extended his left hand in the direction of the gym. Flur S. Ence was about to carry out her first assignment.

GONE WITH THE WIND

It was lunchtime before I got wind of what had happened, and then it was only vague rumours that Madame Shoo hadn't been seen at Dim Son's side at the communal breakfast. It was also hinted that there was an unknown, and much younger woman, with him. I would never have identified Flur S. Ence as that woman, but to my horror, that was confirmed later in the day. I had a few hours – blissful in retrospect – where I suspected nothing. Nichts.

Looking back on it, I did sense a strange atmosphere in the galley, not quite a silence; conversations were being transacted in lower frequency whispers, a sign that substantial rumours or concrete speculations had gathered momentum. Being out of touch and self-absorbed in my own world of petty resentments, I dismissed the vibe as more of the same-old-same-old waffle.

Madame Shoo missing from breakfast wasn't necessarily an indication that something momentous had taken place. People get colds, the flu, that sort of thing and, although the same woman was tougher than gnarled blackthorn, she no doubt was as susceptible to the odd virus as the rest of us. Whatever.

I wandered down to the scriptwriters' office on my way back, just a social call so to say, contemplating on Madame Shoo's absence, and little thinking on what the ramifications were for myself. I hadn't twigged a thing up until then but I did raise an eyebrow and my moustaches bristled as I entered. Neither of my scriptwriters were there, and our section of the open plan office was deserted, completely empty. She was missing, Klusch was missing, the typists and admin people were missing. *Nichts*, *Nada*. Must be a meeting, I thought, and in my narcissism, the very next thought was: who the hell is the head of department here and why are meetings being called without my knowledge?

It could only mean one thing: I had been replaced! They've done it this time, I concluded, they've taken me down. Right now the staff are probably being debriefed, the change of leadership is being explained and Vascher is history. Oh woe is me! A chill colder than an eskimo's toilet bowl went right through me; who among us is not afraid of death my friend? But why hadn't they arrested me? I looked around, half imagining a troop of soldiers coming down the corridor, under orders to cart me off to the chute, but there was nobody. I looked over at the other sections; they were all working away and were oblivious to my presence.

I kid you not, but I reversed out of there on tippy toes and made my way back to my cubbyhole, convinced again that I was to be met by an arresting party on route, but the corridor was deserted. God's air. I made my way to my cabin and peeped inside the open door. Just as I left it. No one there either, and no one had been there as far as I could make out. I stepped inside quickly and pulled the door shut behind me and if there had been a lock I would have deployed it there and then.

Nothing to do but wait. And wait I did. Nobody came near me throughout the day. From time to time I stiffened when I heard people moving along the corridor, but not a single person knocked on my door. Maybe they're just cutting off the oxygen, so to say, I thought? Let him find out by stealth that he's been chopped. Maybe he'll do the decent thing himself and finish it forever? Could be, I figured; I'm no longer in *der erste Reihe* and this would not be a completely atypical way to terminate a career – I'd seen the message delivered in stranger ways, believe you me. I hurt my brain trying to rationalise what was going on and finished up dizzy as a Weejy Weejy bird.

To my shame, it took some considerable time before any

thoughts on the welfare of others entered my consciousness, specifically Flur S. Ence. I made a few phone calls. I braved it out onto the stairs again and checked the conference rooms – nothing. I even checked the general office again – nothing. I returned to my office and brooded on what might have happened. Maybe nothing had happened, became the one positive thought, and I hunkered down, my ears on overtime and awaited the dreaded knock, or – unrealistically – the innocent countenance and shy smile of that beautiful young woman, Flur S. Ence.

SQUEEZE YOUR BUM TIME

One of the three young women waved her impatiently away and she moved out of the alcove. As she turned to go, her eyes popped as she saw all three women hoist up their dresses and lower their knickers before settling themselves on the yoga mats. She put her hand to her mouth and went through the revolving doors, leaning on the wall as she reached 'safety'. She could not quite believe what she had just seen as she went through to the locker rooms.

Soon afterwards she heard, but could not identify, the whipping sounds coming from inside. A terrible urge to look in, even to inch the door slightly open, came over her and she had to clinch her hands to resist. The noise, followed by squeals and grunting noises, increased in volume and went on and on. After it quietened a soldier came over and motioned her back into the gym proper. There she found the women rearranging their clothes and chatting amongst themselves.

They passed her by without comment and sized her up, wondering no doubt where Madame Shoo had gotten to. Flur S. Ence knew she was trapped, knew instantly that she had to go along with whatever came her way. She was no different to a house hostage and adducing this, her brain functioned as if she were a prisoner, aligning it with that state of mind. Nothing else could help her in the current dilemma.

The soldier returned and informed her that she was to go and wait at the lifts for Dim Son.

THE NOOSE TIGHTENS

At 19:00 hours a message came by courier that I was required to attend a progress meeting in the conference room by order of Dim Son's office. It was not signed and assuming that it was at Madame Shoo's request, I must confess that it was probably the only time in my miserable life that I looked forward to her presence; it's astonishing what the dearth of information will do to a man's brain.

The message/order also instructed me to have a report on the current status of the project and supporting backup material, including video footage, for presentation at the meeting. Furthermore, I was to supply a detailed synopsis of the budget – actual outlay to date and projected expenditure right up to project completion, deviations from agreed guidelines to be fully explained, along with a coherent and realistic plan on how to re-align.

Well, *vielen Dank mein Freund!* Do you think I have nothing to do? I jested to myself, but inside blue panic, in the form of breathy sighs and tugs of moustaches, broke out in an all-consuming and very personal riot. Slow the breathing, *immer langsam mit der Ruhe*, I commanded myself. *Scheiße!* None of that malarkey worked. I gave myself over to a plague of half-thoughts as my thrashing CPU continued to produce the square root of fuck all.

The bitch has me; she has got hold of my team and has installed herself as the maestro, but she'll be subtle - no doubt about it. I could just see it; I'll get enough rope to hang myself and then they'll pounce. I haven't a bull's notion what the budget is – nor do I give a donkey's curse – and as far as the project itself... well I can't bluff my way through that, not now.

Hand on heart, I have hardly looked at those details since the *verdammt Ding* was approved. Flur S. Ence has all of that and her desk has been cleared of everything down to the last erasers. I'll be totally exposed when asked to deliver my report. Oh, well planned, you anorexic bitch, I'll give you that... I tip my sombrero.

I'll be reduced to a blabbering embarrassment; they'll look around, casting sad and regretful eyes in my direction, and then in with the knife, pushing home the Mackie Messer and twisting it in. His Blobness will turn to the Shepherd's Crook beside him and give the nod, his flab rolling with delight. At last, they have got Vascher and another one of Daddy Kühl's cohorts bites the dust. Of course herself will see it as the crowning achievement of her Richelieu reign, the fly in the ointment finally creamed, but she'll do it with delicate words, gently telling me to go to hell and have me look forward to the trip.

A long list of the non-deliverables will be served up, people will cringe at my sins of omission and they will assert that a great catastrophe has been avoided at the last minute. People will push forward in their chairs, clamouring, 'get rid of him - *for God's sake*, get rid of him before he does more damage.'

I admit I haven't helped my own cause – what cause was that again? – and a plethora of mismanaged FUBARs are scattered in my wake; carelessness and incompetence will be added to the deficit ledger. '*Get rid of him,*' the mantra will repeat, so that in the end when she turns around and displays my severed head to the crowd they will applaud her compassion.

Just imagine my surprise (horror!) when they came in. Himself *and* Flur S. Ence; not a sign of Madame Shoo. I kept looking around waiting for her, thinking maybe that they were going to throw me out before she made her grand entrance, ready as ever to save the kingdom from the useless oaf who had whittled away the resources under his command. But appear she did not and the galley rumours came back to me with a thump.

They were all there – I mean my crew – all of them, including my old adversary, Klusch, looking somewhat puzzled I must add, the only thing that gave me a sliver of hope. What's going on, I thought? I really hadn't a clue. My musing came to a halt as Flur S. Ence cleared her throat.

'Chief Boddle Vascher, Dim Son requests that you deliver your status report as requested.'

I could see myself rising from my chair, a separate entity, almost in slow motion, and I adjusted my trousers and checked that my moustaches were still attached. My physical movements had slowed down and my brain was moving at glacial speed, while at the same time, in a strange way, I sensed that I had all the time in the world. I pulled myself up to my nosebleed height of one meter fifty and cleared my throat in an echo of Flur S. Ence's introduction.

'Thank you Flur S. Ence. Forgive me for not adding a title since I am not informed of the changes that have manifested in the previous 24 hours.'

There was a shuffle of people on their seats; it was 'squeeze your bum' time. The last thing on my mind was to make life more difficult for my erstwhile protégée, but where the hell was Madame Shoo? What was this humiliating act they were putting Flur S. Ence and myself through?

'With the utmost regret, I wish to inform the meeting, and let the protocol record this,' I added, with a stern look in Klusch's direction, who nearly departed his chair for a second time (I jest!), 'that certain prerequisites need to be adhered to before a full and comprehensive report can be submitted to what I presume is an EGM. Since I have had neither the resources nor the time to produce said report, I must now, in full view of the collected assembly, decline the opportunity to appraise you of the aforesaid at this present moment in time. I will go further,' here I raised my head, summoning as much gravitas as I could as I scanned the room, 'and with utmost seriousness, declare that it would be an unforgivable breach of national security were I to do so.'

Whether I knew it, or whether he knew it, I was taking him on, and those present were instinctively aware of this; you could slice the atmosphere with a Yokohama hommer. I wasn't quite sure whether His Plumpness was picking this up, for I had left Terra Firma several minutes earlier, and I wasn't too concerned whether he was or whether he wasn't.

Flur S. Ence it was who broke the charged silence. In their fear, I was fully convinced that the others at the meeting, with the possible exception of the main players, wanted to leap up as one and tear me to pieces. Fair play to that slip of a girl, she hadn't let her fear – and she must have been close to wetting herself – get in the way of a low-key response.

'What do you need to prepare and present your report, Chief Boddle Vascher?'

Good question, I said to myself. We're batting on opposite sides of a sticky wicket; hard, low ground hurling. Her question gave me a platform, or should I say, her question empowered me to take a further step up the celestial ladder.

'Thank you for your question Flur S. Ence. Very simply, I require the following: my team returned to me forthwith; all my materials - including works in progress - made available to me; furthermore, I require a full working week to put the requested report together. Now I say a week, but I would be most gracious if some flexibility could be extended in this regard, as one knows, matters are complicated, unforeseen events intrude, etc. Shall we say… a month?'

Flur S. Ence repeated my demands with a straight bat while I remained standing at Silly Mid Off.

'Oh, by the way,' and here I decided to hurl a rasper down the wing, 'Madame Shoo has been an intimate in this production from the outset and is the possessor of information which I deem relevant, absolutely essential indeed, if the tasks as outlined are to be given their proper due diligence.'

There was no reply from Flur S. Ence this time round and I allowed myself a glance in Dim Son's direction. He was sitting side on at the table, being too damn big to sit face on, slouching without intent and as vacant as ever; it was almost as if he wasn't there, and perhaps he wasn't.

There followed a short lull in proceedings and being unwilling to be the saviour of countenance for anyone, I bowed deeply and sat back down. Flur S. Ence whispered briefly in Dim Son's ear, pointed at his chief guard, and called the meeting to an end. There immediately followed a mass exodus in the wake of the Waddling Weenie and his guards.

TEAMWORK

Flur S. Ence remained seated, and after the others had moved out into the corridor she rose and closed the door gently. She didn't look at me as she took her seat again at the table and concentrated intently on a sheaf of documents before her. I had the distinct impression that she wanted me to say something, but what could I say? I was completely in the dark and fighting for my very existence, no exaggerating. Eventually I did open my mouth to ask a question.

'What's going on?' I put it as plainly as I could.

She moved slightly, as if to say why ask me. I waited.

'I am the stand in for Madame Shoo... as far as I can tell.'

My thinking hadn't got me that far and I was relieved that I didn't know it when I made my rebellious speech from the dock. So that was it. Madame Shoo was out of the picture. Benign or malign – who knew?

'Go on,' I almost barked, curiosity getting the better of me.

This time she looked directly at me; her eyes reprimanded me for the display of verbal aggression which I acknowledged by raising my left hand in an apologetic gesture.

'She is indisposed, that is the line I've been given.'

Indisposed, I conjectured. To chute or not to chute, that is the supplementary question.

'I've been installed in her place,' she continued, 'and all evidence of her previous occupation has been wiped away. It is as if she never existed.'

There was a catch in her voice and I could see the dismay in her face. She was trapped and would have to serve too until she was cast aside and appeared never to have existed. I imagined for a fleeting second the drudgery of the scriptwriters' office was freedom compared to where she had landed.

Funnily enough, I took encouragement from her spoken and unspoken communication. Why, you ask? Very simply because I could see that I had not lost my Flur. The situation and circumstances had changed and both of us would have to act accordingly and, with that in mind, I opened up to her and proposed a collaborative approach.

'You will have to double job, you know that?'

She nodded and I felt even better seeing her relax a little

and saw the colour return to her face.

'But first I've got to give Dim Son a believable scenario.'

'Don't worry about that,' I interjected, 'we'll work something out, but... tell me – what's the real story with Madame Shoo?'

'Are you obsessed with her?' she asked and I could swear I saw the trace of a smile on her lips.

'You're absolutely right; I've got to keep myself in check – never mind.'

'The truth is, I don't know. I doubt if she has been executed; that has a way of leaking out.'

We continued chatting in this vein for another five or ten minutes, getting to know each other again post all the changes; feeling each other out. I must admit I really enjoyed it – *fabelhaft* – as I had not experienced, up until that moment, a more laid-back conversation with Flur S. Ence. We knew we were centimetres from disaster if we didn't play our cards carefully; we were heading towards endgame and we had to get down to work.

Thanks to Flur S. Ence we had a script, robust enough at this stage, for the re-launch. I had no idea until we started to go through it just how much effort she had put in. Modesty forbids me from mentioning my own contributions – the big picture, the strategy, the denouement, the tension, the character arc, the conflict, the pacy story line, the crisp dialogue… I could go on but that would be bragging and that's just not me.

'The trick is getting the focus moved away from our combined contribution altogether,' I said, 'although – as you and I know – Production is rather picky when taking stuff over from Creative. Want everything on a plate.'

She raised her hand, putting an instant halt to my long-winded, obstacle-oriented train of thought.

'I really think we have to keep it down to the bare bones,' she said, 'nothing too fancy, just deliver what they've been asked for; worrying about what the others do or don't do will just waste our time.'

'Right again,' I replied.

'Okay, you now need to go through the draft and finalise it.'

'Yes,' I mumbled, clear hesitation in my voice, a hesitation which got an almost Madame Shoo type stare.

'I do have another job as well you know?' she frowned.

'Yes, yes,' I backed off, 'absolutely correct. *Einverstanden*,' and for a second time I raised my hand in an apologetic gesture.

'So that's it taken care of. All we need now is the budget summary.' A revitalised, assertive woman was manifesting before me and I winced, fearful that she might delegate it to me – I hate budgets with a vengeance – but instead she gave me a wink and a pass. No, not that type of pass!

'No worries, I'll take care of it; Madame Shoo's spreadsheets have been handed over to me. And that's where I must go now; it's hard to credit the extent of her responsibilities,' she concluded as she left me, open-mouthed and gob smacked all at once.

So I had got it all wrong. True, something had happened and the rumours emanating from the canteen did have a solid foundation, but all subsequent speculation by my good self had been off the mark; Madame Shoo, or more specifically, her fate, was a mystery, but there was no doubting who had replaced her – temporarily or permanently – and who was now my de facto boss. Strange as it may sound to you, I didn't have a problem with it. I am well aware of my ego's fragility, but when it came to a move like that, coupled with the known facts, I felt comparatively at ease. This could all work out. Flur S. Ence had confided in me – and she had to have her own self-preservation in mind before doing so.

Our script was hot, full of brio and tuned perfectly to the target audience. Yes, I grant you that we are talking about an audience of one, but please hold fire until you see what we have cooked up. It is my contention – for those with eyes to see and brains to analyse – that we captured the complete story of KRAK, and it certainly wasn't a paean to the Dim Dynasty. Yes, that was in there and we were also truthful to the legacy; there were some fine policies in Daddy Kühl's early days; but also in there, disguised in plain sight, was the current reality and the denouement of the whole edifice... *und der Absturz war auch klar zu sehen.*

GIRL POWER

In her most pessimistic moments Flur S. Ence had feared a work-to-rule response from Vascher, but no, he had rowed in immediately. He may not have known it, but Chief Boddle Vascher with his eccentricity, his oddball creativity and his healthy scepticism, had a profound impact on her, and now she was managing a position that in other circumstances would have overwhelmed her. There was something else starting to develop; she was been drawn closer to the emotional life of Vascher, something she had definitely not seen coming and she laughed like a little girl at the thought.

Her new role, she learned early on, was anything but straightforward and her discipline and observation helped to just about keep her head above water in the court of Dim Son. A world turned upside down, inverted in a way that would try a person twice her age, yet she coped, coped better than she ever expected. A capacity to attend to people - whether it be the cleaning staff or the gym girls, the cooks or the guards, the diplomats or the generals, even Dim Son himself - stood to her.

By a large margin, he was her greatest challenge and, as was the case with Madame Shoo, she had to predict what he really wanted, since he never knew himself. She had adapted quickly and initial stumbles had for the most part been eradicated, even if it was a case of Russian roulette much of the time.

However, and it is no stain on Flur S. Ence's stellar performance, despite her almost heroic transformation, Dim Son himself had not adjusted to the change in quite the same way; in fact he was struggling. The problem could be summed up in two words: Madame Shoo.

A chemical balance, the import of which went unnoticed and indeed undiagnosed, had become evident in even more bizarre behaviour than heretofore; he took to the bed during the day and wandered the corridors of a deserted Ritz at night, waking and unsettling the night guards.

He stopped asking about Vascher's project, which ironically enough was making real progress and, after it was all over, would be regarded as an important historical document in the relatively short history of that entity known as KRAK (*Ed.* It is one of the primary sources for what you read here). In its place, Dim Son's obsession shifted to the SCUT-r rocket technology.

And what a disaster (in some peoples' eyes at least) that turned out to be.

General Stab was probably most to blame having, under pressure, shown the dictator where the 'real' prototype rocket was cleverly hidden inside the Ritz's mock funnel and once seen, Dim Son could not rest until the thing was ready to be put to use.

'Are we there yet?' he would ask Flur S. Ence each and every morning and, in compliance with her master's order she would dutifully request a meeting with the general.

The general, a gentleman from his rows of medals to his polished boot tops, bowed on entering her office, causing her some embarrassment, but she was getting used to it by now. He came immediately to the point.

'What can I do, can *you* tell me?' and on her negative shake of the head he proceeded to explain Dim Son's insistence that the missile be launched immediately after the opening episode of the new DDT series.

'Can we do that?' she asked

'The simple answer is no we cannot, but he won't take No for an answer. We need more time.'

'Have you explained that to him?'

General Stab looked at her as if he were about to leap out of his seat and for the first time she saw a frisson of temper on the round face.

'Of course I have, again and again – but he won't listen!'

'How much time do you need?'

'I don't know!'

Flur S. Ence moved in her chair. She had no need to ask the general any more questions – the implications of Dim Son's insistence were clear. The general rose and before he left, uttered a somewhat fatalistic statement: 'I am a soldier, I serve, I take orders. I have no choice.' And then he was gone.

ALL THINGS MUST PASS

The Ritz in its entirety collapsed in on itself one fine day, taking with it the crescent bridge underneath. All that remained were two leaning pillars at either end, like the enormous stubs of rotten old teeth. Don't ask me how, perhaps the depth of stone underneath wasn't strong enough for Daddy Kühl's over-generous statement of opulence.

There were other rumours, not least that the rocket scientists in the basement had messed around with the alarm systems for one of their 'tests'. Whatever. The whole thing came tumbling down, tons and tons of masonry falling in on itself leaving a sky high ash cloud that hung around for days; a sarcophagus for interred vanity.

No Survivors! was the lurid headline in the Yellow Press across the border, but even wilder rumours started to take off immediately, one of which had Dim Son riding around in the Blue Mountains on a luminous white stallion and another, possibly less fanciful, that he had taken off in the SCUT-r.

KRAK never quite made it as far as Mighty; scuttled by a crack in the natural structure which brought down the layers of intrigue, cruelty and the evil of our species. Yours and mine, my friend.

We *weren't* in the Ritz on the evening that the earth shook. You remember my friend Sepp Seife, *Ja*? I had visited him in Slag City and you may recall that he wasn't looking that well at the time. I didn't know it but my poor *Kumpel* had advanced cancer; he knew it, but for his own reasons, had decided not to tell me. Anyway, the old network was capable of getting a message of his passing to me and I was, as you will well imagine, not going to miss the funeral of my departed friend. By the merest of coincidents Flur S. Ence finished up coming along with me. Let me explain.

Flur S. Ence in her new capacity had the authority to issue the *Genehmigung* for passes to and from the Ritz Corral – I was issued with a *Carte Blanche* and there was no need to bribe a van driver! Anyway, when I explained my reasons for heading down to Slag, she asked if I would mind if she came along. I had no objections and as you have surely fathomed, I enjoyed her company. Her reason for coming was nothing to do with Sepp – she didn't know the man – but she had a deep desire to see her elderly parents and had a fear that being in Dim Son's entourage might prevent her ever seeing them again (state secrets and all that).

Little did either of us think as we made our way out in the official limo that we were leaving the Ritz for the last time. Sepp would have laughed loudly to know that his funeral coincided with the implosion of the festering palace on the hill.

In the confusion that followed the explosion (we felt the shock waves as we were singing a bawdy version of *l'Internationale* in The Rising Son). Flur S. Ence and myself finished up staying at her parents apartment for several days. Anarchy was not long in taking hold and the streets became dangerous. Supplies, including basic foodstuffs, became harder and harder to get hold of. Luckily Flur S. Ence's parents were shopkeepers and we had enough to get by, but we had to defend it.

Never again do I wish to be in the position where I had to let off shotgun cartridges over the heads of rioters, but that is what I had to do on one occasion, scattering a mob who went off searching for easier prey. Later that same day, a rumour spread that there was treasure galore in the depths of the gorge wherein the Ritz now lay and the horde surged off in that direction. Unfortunately for them the Siouxer river which had been banked up by the remains of the Ritz, burst through, drowning several hundred looters as it swept down and flooded the low-lying port area of Slag City.

A well-drilled and disciplined army is an asset in those circumstances, and a conclave of colonels, led by General Stab, whose big head appeared every evening in the news bulletins, instituted emergency laws, put soldiers on the streets, cleared up the mess and eventually brought an eerie quiet back to the capital.

Everything was far from stable of course, but an endurable status quo of near normality emerged. I made long distance calls to Erika, giving her what details I could and I discovered, not surprisingly in hindsight, that those on the outside knew more about happenings in KRAK than we did. How can I ever thank my dear Erika. She worked night and day on my behalf and came up trumps about six weeks after the collapse. A supply ship, part of the international aid effort, was due to drop off foodstuffs at the port in a week or two and she had arranged to have my diplomatic status recognised and this enabled me to get on board.

EPILOGUE

Well, my friend, if you have stayed with me this long, then I believe the time has come to release you from your dutiful, and sincerely appreciated, perseverance. I thank you - yes, Chief Boddle Vascher's modesty has swelled in his latter years; you might even say when it comes to humility he is the very tops. Mein lieber mann! Chief no more, just plain ol' Boddle at your service these days.

We settled down, Flur S. Ence and I, in a small hamlet just south of *Schicki-Micki* city. Erika, my sister, lives within walking distance and will be over later on for lunch. Life is good, I have to say. Do I miss the excitement and shenanigans? A little I suppose, but you might say I have reached the age of serenity; happy to see out the rest of my days without some endless *Scheinkrieg* to bother me any longer. I walk the dog; I go down to the *Stammtisch*; I tend the garden – intermittently – and Flur S. Ence is a magnificent cook, so I am well fed and, while never a shrinking *Veilchen*, my waistline has expanded by some centimetres since those last days in KRAK.

Those were the days my friend, we thought they'd never end but, in common with all earthly phenomena, they did. Like children being called in from play, the demise of Daddy Kühl had brought me down with a bang and, after sipping the vintages at his table, I was back out on the slopes sweating at the harvest, with that voracious wolf, Dim Son, shadowing my existence. No matter. The two women in my life, Flur S. Ence and Erika, I owe everything to. Without Erika we could never have made it out and without Flur S. Ence I would most certainly have gone a whistling down the chute.

There was just one thing: Flur S. Ence. Oh, silly old Vascher, you fell in love; how could you leave her? I knew I couldn't, so we did the obvious thing. I was steeped to have my love returned and she made the tough decision to join me and bid farewell to her native land. It must be noted that it did not come without pain for Flur as she had to make what might be a final goodbye to her parents (it wasn't, for which I thank the good Lord). Flur now works as a Media Studies lecturer in *Angeberstadt* and she has had a number of plays published, both here and abroad. And to her success I now raise my glass of

Chivas Regal and salute her, my life companion and saviour.

Bis demnächst!

APPENDIX

German Translations

Translations are not always literal and are designed to transfer the intent of the phrase.

Page 12	*Wo sind wir denn hier?*	- What's going on?
Page 17	*Hellkopf*	- Smartass
Page 17	*begeistert*	- impressed, excited
Page 18	*Ach mein Junge*	- My dear boy
Page 18	*Hund*	- Dog
Page 18	*Verdammt auch das noch*	- Damn it, that as well
Page 18	*Mein Freund*	- My friend
Page 18	*Außer Spesen nichts gewesen*	- A business jolly
Page 19	*Brauerei*	- Brewery
Page 26	*Ausgezeichnet*	- Excellent
Page 26	*Zeitlupe... entsch...*	- Slow motion... excus...
Page 32	*schmeichelhaft*	- Flattering
Page 33	*Jawoll*	- Yes sir (ironical)
Page 43	*Laß es sein Vascher!*	- Let it be Vascher!
Page 44	*Drei verdammte Monate*	- Three damn months
Page 45	*Meine Güte*	- My goodness
Page 45	*Darstellung*	- Presentation

Page 45/6	*Spitzel*	- Spy
Page 46	*Hintergrund*	- Background
Page 52	*Genau*	- Exactly
Page 59	*um Gottes willen!*	- For God's sake!
Page 84	*Scheiße, absolut Scheiße*	- Shite, absolute shite
Page 84	*GewerkshaftderArschlecker*	- The asslickers' union
Page 84	*Wessie*	- Someone from West Germany
Page 84	*Grüne Insel*	- Ireland
Page 84	*Lebenskünstler*	- A bit of a character
Page 85	*Lebenslauf*	- CV, resumé
Page 92	*Kneipe*	- Bar
Page 93	*Stammtisch*	- Regulars' table (in a bar)
Page 103	*Echt, absolut Furcht*	- The truth, absolute fear
Page 103	*Verstehst Du jetzt?*	- Do you understand now?
Page 103	*nicht wahr?*	- True?
Page 103	*richtig*	- Correct
Page 104	*Die zweite Reihe*	- Middle management
Page 104	*Das glaube ich nicht*	- I don't believe it
Page 104	*Frechheit*	- Devilment
Page 116	*Verdammter Wächter*	- Damned sentry/guard
Page 117	*ach, mein Kopf*	- Oh, my poor head
Page 119	*verdammt Klug, die junge Frau*	- Damn smart, that young woman
Page 123	*echt Eisen*	- Real iron
Page 124	*bitte!*	- If you please!
Page 138	*das hat gedauert*	- That took a while
Page 139	*Gleichgültigkeit*	- Indifference

Page 139	*Apfelschorle* - non-alcoholic apple drink
Page 140	*Verdammte Hexe* - Damned witch
Page 141	*Verdammter Roman* - A damned novel
Page 143	*bist Du klug oder was?* - Who's a clever boy?
Page 153	*Mackie Messer* - Mack The Knife
Page 156	*immer mit der Ruhe* - Now, take it nice and easy
Page 157	*wie ein frisch geborenes Kind* - Like a newborn babe
Page 157	*Kanonendonner ist mein Gruß!* - Canon fire is my greeting!
Page 167	*schaffe, schaffe* - Work, work
Page 172	*ach mein alter Spion* - Ah! my good old spy
Page 173	*Arschloch* - Asshole
Page 187	*ganz richtig* - Quite correct
Page 189	*In Ordnung…Du hast Recht* - Agreed… you are right
Page 195	*Vernichtung* - Extermination
Page 195	*Jein* - Yes and no
Page 195	*Stets nach dem letzten Motto* - As commanded
Page 195	*Alles… ich habe Glück gehabt* - All in all… I was lucky
Page 202	*Mein alter Kumpel* - My old mate
Page 203	*das war herrlich* - That was wonderful
Page 204	*Dankbarkeit* - Gratitude
Page 212	*Besprechung under vier Augen* - Private conversation, tête-à-tête
Page 219	*Nichts* - Nothing
Page 220	*Der erste Reihe* - In the forefront, top of the class
Page 225 (ironic)	*Vielen Dank mein Freund* - Many thanks my friend
Page 225	*immer langsam mit der Ruhe* - Take it easy!

Page 225	*Scheiße* - Shit
Page 225	*verdammt Ding* - Damned thing
Page 233	*fabelhaft* - Fabulous
Page 234	*einverstanden* - I agree
Page 236	*der Absturz war auch klar zu sehen* - The downfall was also clear to see
Page 242	*Genehmigung* - Approval
Page 245	*Schikimicki* - Trendy, arrogant
Page 246	*Scheinkrieg* - Phoney war
Page 247	*Angeberstadt* - Show off city
Page 247	*Bis demnächst!* - Until the next time!

Printed in Poland
by Amazon Fulfillment
Poland Sp. z o.o., Wrocław